HERMANOS

Sebastian I

Always late.

13 year old Sebastian Gonzalez raced downhill on his bike, his stomach tied up in knots. He thought of his older brother, Jorge, and his presumed reaction to Sebastian's tardiness.

He's gonna get onto me again.

Not that it was entirely undeserved of course. This was the third day in a row that he'd be getting home after curfew and today was an especially important day.

He looked down at his watch.

7:25.

He hadn't intended on losing track of time at Raul's house but one second he had time to spare and the next he was 5 minutes behind schedule. Now it was up to 25.

The sun had already begun to set and dusk was settling in, yet the Texas heat was still as intense as ever.

Of all the days, Sebastian. Of all the days.

Now he was chastising himself.

It was the one year anniversary of his mother's death and here he was, pedaling his heart out, trying to get home for the brothers' personal memorial.

Their dad had been gone a year after his youngest brother, Abel, was born. Then, a year ago, when Jorge was 20, Sebastian was 12, and Abel was 9, their mother passed away from breast cancer.

Now all the three brothers had left was each other.

All that's left is us. Sebastian thought to himself. *And I'm still late!*

Their mom had left a little money for them, thanks to a decent life insurance. That wouldn't last forever, though, so Jorge took it upon himself to become the breadwinner, lest the brothers be separated and the youngest sent to foster care.

Now to add insult to injury he had recently been let go from his job.

A pang of guilt hit Sebastian's chest.

All that Jorge does for me and I can't even make it home on time.

His brother could be naggy and temperamental sometimes, but he knew that everything he did was for them. The least he could do is make it home in time for requiems.

As he continued to pedal, the house came into view. It was a depressing sight as all the lights remained off aside from one to the left.

The light to his mother's room.

He reached the fence and hopped off his bike, up onto the porch and to the front door.

Abel opened it before he had even reached the doorknob.

"Hurry up!" His little brother said, ushering him inside.

"I know, I know, I'm sorry."

They ran down the hall, into their mother's room.

"Jorge I'm sorry, I didn't even look at my watch, I didn't mean to-"

He stopped as his older brother looked up at him. Their eyes met and Sebastian could see Jorge's were red with tears. In his lap he held a photo album, currently open to a picture from Abel's 5th birthday party.

A cake in front of them, the small family was huddled together, smiling and laughing. Abel's little face was covered in icing, Jorge stood with a napkin trying to get him clean, and Sebastian had his arm around his mother's shoulder.

Teardrops fell to the plastic cover over the photos as Sebastian sat down next to Jorge on the bed.

"I'm sorry I'm late." He said, leaning his head onto his big brother's shoulder.

Abel sat on the other side. He too rested his head.

"It's ok." Jorge said, his voice cracked with sadness.

He closed the photo album and opened it to the first page again.

They began to flip through.

__Jorge I__

This job interview was not going well.

Jorge shifted nervously in his seat as he bombed question after question.

It wasn't so much due to the quality of his answers, rather the interviewer was clearly disinterested in anything he had to say. The laughs emanating from the room just before Jorge had entered, and as the previous interviewee had exited, were now replaced by the stern tone of a man who had already made his choice for employee.

Jorge's interview was simply a formality and that made him especially anxious. All this experience was doing was reminding him of why he had such trouble with authority figures.

I wouldn't even have to be here if Teresa hadn't kicked me to the curb. 3 years of hard work meant nothing apparently.

His former boss, the aforementioned Teresa, had let him go without much fanfare or notice.

"I need this job." He had pleaded. "More than you know. Please, I have my two brothers and-"

Teresa had held her hand up to silence him.

"I'm sorry kid, I really am. I know things have been tough for you lately, what with your mother and stuff, but I can't keep you around. I'm sorry. I would if I could but cuts have to be made."

And with that he was fired.

Now, here he was making a fool of himself during an interview for a job he wasn't going to get. How embarrassing to not even be able to get hired for cart pushing duties.

He had no problem being hired at a grocery store, but it admittedly stung a little to be flopping so bad.

"Well then," Mr. Jackson said, clearly ending the interview, "we'll call you if we feel you're the right fit."

With that, Jorge got up and, head hung low, walked back to his beat up 2005 Explorer. In the front seat he slumped against the steering wheel.

He could feel his breathing beginning to speed up. His hand shook.

Panic attack. He thought to himself.

They had been occurring more frequently lately. First they had started after his mother's death and they were pretty bad. Within a couple months he managed to get them a bit more under control, mostly for the sake of his brothers.

He wanted to be strong for them.

Then, when he got fired, they returned with a vengeance.

His head swirled with anxiety as he felt himself disassociating.

Car. You're in the car. Calm down and look around. You see the store. You feel the steering wheel in your hand. You smell the air freshener. You can hear the other cars passing by. Taste...what do you taste?

He breathed in and out. He still felt anxious and disconnected but it had subsided a bit. Though he had wanted to try therapy, there just wasn't that kind of extra money lying around.

The only tips he had learned for controlling his panic attacks had been thanks to Google and YouTube.

He took out his phone and clicked to call Sebastian.

"Hello?" His brother answered.

"Hey Seb, I'm gonna be headed home now. Do y'all want something quick? Like McDonalds?"

"Hold up." Jorge heard the phone move from Sebastian's face. "ABEL!"

No response.

"ABEL!!!!"

"WHAT?"

"JORGE WANTS TO KNOW IF YOU WANT SOMETHING FROM MCDONALDS!!!!"

"MCDONALDS?"

"YEAH!"

"YEAH A 10 PIECE NUGGETS!"

Sebastian returned to the call. "Yeah Abel wants a 10 piece nuggets and I want a Big Mac."

"Ok," Jorge answered. "You know instead of yelling you could've just walked to his room."

His brother laughed. "Where's the fun in that?"

Jorge smiled. The boys were chaotic but that's what he loved most about them. They seemed to be the only shining parts of his life anymore.

"Alright, well I'll see y'all when I get there. Are Dr. Peppers okay?"

"Hold on let me check-"

"Nah nah nah, I'll just get that." Jorge said with a chuckle. "No need to yell more. I'll be there soon."

"Alright bye."

-Click-

He set down the phone and began to pull out of the parking lot. His stomach still felt a bit knotted from the panic attack but he was getting over it.

You have to be strong. Strong for them.

The words echoed in his mind. They weren't just a mantra that he used to remind himself. They had been his mother's last words.

With her final breath she had left him with a responsibility he'd have to carry with himself for the rest of his life.

I promise, mom. I promise I will.

The words had escaped his mouth in bursts. The tears streamed down his face as he had held onto her hand.

It wasn't long before her breathing ceased.

For her. I'm doing this for her.

He continued thinking for a beat.

And for them.

He looked over to a photo of the three brothers clipped onto his car visor.

All smiles. Not knowing what the future was about to hit them with. It was taken 3 months before their mother's diagnosis.

They had taken a trip to Guadalajara to visit their grandmother. It was hectic, but looking back it had also been so much fun.

Someday we'll get back to that.

Abel I

"He's not getting out of bed today, is he?"

Sebastian shook his head as he closed the door to Jorge's room. " I don't think so."

This happened sometimes. Jorge had what his brothers like to call "Gone Days". He'd slip into a depression and lay in bed all day, not to be seen until the next.

"What caused this?" Abel asked, following Sebastian down the hall.

"I think the people from the job interview called him to say they were going with someone else. He had already seemed kinda down yesterday when he got back and now with the confirmation..."

Poor Jorge. Abel thought to himself as the boys entered the kitchen.

He loved his brother with all his heart and it hurt to see him on a Gone Day. Jorge was his hero and he wanted to be exactly like him when he grew up.

Just as tough as him.

His stomach growled. Sebastian looked over from the fridge. "You hungry?"

"Yeah." Abel answered. "What's there for breakfast."

"Well, lets see. Maybe some toast since we have...wait, nevermind the bread is expired."

He lobbed the loaf into the air and made it directly into the trash can.

"Ok let's see," Sebastian said, opening the pantry, "hmmmm. Not very many options to be honest."

Abel placed his hand atop his stomach. "Anything will do. What about some microwaveable meals? Was there any in the fridge?"

"Nope. Sorry."

Sebastian pulled a can of beans from the sad pantry. "Not really breakfast food but this is about the best I can offer. This or noodles."

Abel thought it over. "I guess the beans."

He watched as the middle brother worked his way around the kitchen, first to find a can opener, then a small pot and finally to the stove.

It began to heat up as he grabbed a chair to sit down.

I miss mom.

Their mother was a fiery woman who always worked magic with whatever little food they had. Abel recalled waking up in the morning to the gorgeous smells of her Mexican cooking.

The sounds of her music drifted up with the aromas and his stomach would growl at the anticipation. He'd sprint to his favorite seat at the table.

"Look who's up first." His mother would say with a smile. "Ten mi gordito."

Abel smiled at the memory.

I loved being her 'gordito'. Even if it was a little bit of an insult.

It was true though. He was both the youngest and chunkiest of the brothers. He was overweight, more...shapely than his slim and lanky older brothers.

Gordito was a...wait what did Jorge say that one time? A term of endearment! That was it.

Sure it was basically a cute way of saying fatty, but now that she was gone he missed it more than ever.

"Okie dokie." Sebastian said, scooping some beans out onto a small plastic bowl. "Bon appétit, hermano."

He grabbed the bowl from his brother and, spoon already in hand, dug in.

It's not pancakes, Abel thought, *but it'll do.*

"I think I'm gonna heat up a tortilla to get full, you gonna want one?"

Abel nodded his head. "And maybe a little more beans?"

Sebastian looked into the pan on the stove. "Yeah I think there's enough for seconds. I wanna leave some for Jorge in case he gets up today."

Oh yeah.

Abel had nearly forgotten his brother, holed up in his dark room.

I hope he's out by later today.

Sebastian sat down at the table, tortillas in hand. "You ok? You look kinda of worried."

Abel sheepishly looked away.

"He's gonna be fine." His brother said, scooping some of his beans onto the tortilla. "You know he gets like this sometimes, but by the next day he's all better. Just gotta have a little faith in him."

"I know. It's just...I don't know, I guess. Sometimes I feel afraid he won't come back out."

Sebastian shook his head. "Don't think like that. You know he wouldn't give up on us, not completely anyways. He just has a lot he's going through."

He took a bite of his food. "Think about it this way, think about how hard it's been dealing with mom's death right?"

Abel nodded.

"Well," Sebastian continued, "Jorge's not only dealing with all that grief and sadness, he's also dealing with having to provide for us. Hell, school starts in a month! We're gonna need our uniforms, supplies, extra food to be able to take for lunch, list goes on and on."

He paused for a moment.

"Basically the point I'm making is that he's trying, ok?"

Abel moved his beans around with his spoon.

He's trying, don't be ungrateful. And you have to try too.

"I just want him to be ok."

A wistful look crossed Sebastian's face. "Yeah me too."

They continued to eat in silence.

***

That evening, Jorge finally emerged from his room.

Abel watched as his older brother slunk to the kitchen. Emotionless and with red, tear stained eyes.

"Hey Jorge?"

No answer.

He got up and walked to the kitchen. His oldest brother sat eating at the table.

"Sebastian went out to Raul's house, he said he'd be back before nine."

Jorge nodded slowly.

"Is there anything you need?" Abel asked.

He shook his head no.

"Okay, well I'll be in the living room. Let me know if you need something."

As Abel turned to leave, his brother spoke.

"Wait."

Jorge motioned for Abel to come over. His older brother pulled him in and held him close.

"I'm sorry." He said, his voice weak and hoarse. "I'm sorry I didn't come out today."

Abel stood motionless in his brother's arms. Slowly he wrapped his arms around him.

"It's ok, I know you're trying."

Jorge began to sob into his little brother's shoulder. "I'm sorry you have to see me like this. I'm failing you and Seb. I made a promise to mom and I can't even keep to it. I can't even get a job."

"No, no. It's ok. I know all this is hard for you." Abel said, holding him tightly. "I know how hard you try."

Sebastian II

When Sebastian was 3 years old his mother had found a small gray kitten outside their home, dirty, cold, and trembling.

She brought it in, cleaned it up, and even went out that very day to buy it kitten food.

"Your name," she said, lifting the kitten close to her face, "will be Paz."

Spanish for peace.

Although (seeing as he was only 3 at the time) Sebastian had no memory of this, it was a story he had loved hearing as he grew up.

Jorge, who at that point was 11, remembered that day perfectly and often regaled him with stories of Paz's early days.

Now, ten years later, Paz was getting on in years.

She had been pretty active by cat standards, but by this point she often lounged around the house, sleeping most of the days away.

While Paz was the responsibility of everyone in the house, Sebastian was her favorite.

If she saw him sitting on the sofa she'd jump into his lap, rubbing her head against his chest until he'd pet her.

"Hey pretty girl." He'd say, scratching her lightly underneath her chin. "Somebody's feeling good today."

She'd purr contently until she fell asleep, snuggled closely against him.

Then one day, she started shaking.

A frantic call to Jorge and a rush to the vet's office revealed that she was suffering from neurological issues and her days may be limited.

C'mon pretty girl. Pull through for us.

Once she was home from the vet Sebastian spoiled her beyond belief. Checking on her often, giving her treats, carrying her to bed.

The shaking continued but seemed manageable.

"Hey Seb?"

Sebastian looked up to see Jorge standing over him as he finished laying Paz down on the softest blanket he could find.

"Yeah? What's up?"

"Has Paz been doing any better from the shaking or have things been the same?"

"She's been pretty much the same I guess, at least in terms of frequency. I think she's been sleeping a lot more too."

"But you feel her quality of life is ok?"

Sebastian reached down to stroke the back of her head. "I would hope so, she's been very spoiled lately."

"I'm just saying y'know...well if things get really bad you'll let me know right?"

Sebastian paused as his stomach sank.

"You're not trying to imply we put her down or nothing right?"

Jorge stepped closer.

"Seb, I'm not saying that. I just wanna make sure you'll tell me if things get really bad with her. She's an old cat and if things get too tough it'd be cruel to force her to keep going."

"I won't have her put down."

"And I won't do it if you think that's the wrong thing to do." His older brother said, resting his hand on Sebastian's shoulder. "Just keep an eye on her ok?"

Jorge exited and Sebastian pulled the cat close.

Don't worry girl, I won't give up on you.

The next week passed by without incident until, one day, Sebastian returned home to find Jorge and Abel looking very concerned.

"What's going on?" He asked, tossing his bike helmet to the sofa.

"Seb we need to talk about Paz."

Sebastian felt his stomach drop like a rock. "What do you mean? What happened? Is she okay?"

"She's really struggling lately, especially today. Abel found her earlier, unconscious near her own vomit."

"Wait what?! We have to get her to the vet!"

As Sebastian tried to rush to find her, Jorge stood up and stopped him.

"I called her already. She says if we bring her in she's just gonna recommend euthanasia."

The color drained from Sebastian's face.

"No." He said, his voice shaky. "We can't do that, I'm not gonna give up on her."

"Seb it's not-"

"Stop. I'm not gonna listen."

"It's not right for us to-"

He clamped his hands over his ears.

No. I'm not gonna put her down! I'm not!

"Seb." Jorge said, moving his hands from his ears. "Please listen to me. Go see her. She's in your room."

Sebastian backed away from his brothers and made his way over to his bedroom.

There she lay on the bed.

"Hey pretty girl." He sat down beside her and rested his hand on her body.

Her breathing was labored, her eyes remained closed even as her ears perked at the sound of his voice.

"I'm sorry it took me so long to get here. I got distracted at Raul's house like usual and I didn't even know this was going on."

He felt himself shake as he continued to pat her fur.

"I told you I wasn't gonna give up on you and I meant it. I won't. But at the same time, I know you don't feel good. I know things are tough for you."

He leaned down and kissed her head.

Once he was back in the living room, he walked up to Jorge.

"Do what you think is right. I don't wanna be the one to make the decision. I can't be."

"You know what I think is the right decision, correct?"

"Yeah." Sebastian said sadly. "Don't say it though."

***

That night Sebastian dreamed of his mother.

She was in their living room, emaciated and pale, just as she had been towards the end of her life.

In her lap she held Paz as she was now. Just as sickly.

"Mom?"

No response.

"Mom please."

His mother slowly turned her head.

"You. Gave. Up."

He awoke in bed with a jump.

Her words continued to echo through his head. His breathing grew heavy as a sense of fear took him over.

He leaped from his bed and ran to Jorge's room, pushed the door open and flicked on the light.

Jorge sat up, startled.

"Seb? What's wrong, are you ok?"

Sebastian began to cry and climbed onto Jorge's bed.

"I can't let go of Paz! I can't give up on her!"

His brother pulled him close.

"Hey listen, you aren't giving up on her. She's sick, Seb. She can't go on like how she is, it's not living at this point."

"You don't get it. If I give up on Paz it'll be just like how I gave up on mom!"

A confused look crossed Jorge's face.

"Sebastian you didn't give up on mom, she had cancer. Her body couldn't take it anymore..."

"You don't know." Sebastian said through sobs. "You don't know what I did."

Jorge looked down at him. "What are you talking about?"

Sebastian took a deep breath.

"One day, towards the end, you had left the hospital room to go pick up Abel from his friend's house. I stayed with mom. I remember sitting there in the room, staring at her. I felt so bad because she didn't look like mom anymore. She just slept all day and she didn't even really eat. She wasn't mom."

"Yeah I remember. It was like looking at a stranger."

"It was scary. And you were gone so I went over to her and I gave her a kiss on her forehead. Then I leaned in and whispered to her 'It's ok to let go mom.' At the time I thought it was a nice thing to say, but then she passed away that night. I felt so guilty. Like I had given up on her or told her to give up. I felt like I was the reason she died."

"And now you feel like you're doing the same to Paz."

"Yeah. Exactly."

Jorge sighed. "Seb, you weren't the reason mom died. Your words didn't do that. She let go because she couldn't fight anymore. That's not a bad thing, I don't want it to sound like I'm saying she gave up. She fought so hard. But she wasn't living anymore. She was just hanging on."

"Like Paz is now?"

"Unfortunately. That's why, even though it hurts, I think we need to put her down. She's not living anymore."

Tears continued down Sebastian's cheeks. "I know."

"Tomorrow we can take her in. You can be there with her and send her off peacefully. Besides, you're her favorite."

Sebastian smiled through the cries. "Okay."

***

The next day, at the vet's office, the procedure began.

As Sebastian sat next to her, petting her in her final moments, he leaned close to her.

"It's ok to let go." He said.

The light faded from Paz's eyes as she slipped into her eternal slumber.

At peace.

<u>Abel II</u>

"Please can I just go with you? I've been so
bored around here."

"Sorry bro," Sebastian said, slowly closing the
door, "me and Raul have stuff planned."

The door shut and Abel slunk towards the wall.

Thanks a lot Sebastian.

He looked around in boredom, trying to find
something, anything to do.

*Tv? Oh wait the Netflix didn't get paid. WiFi is
still on though.*

He sat down on the sofa and pulled over
Jorge's laptop which he allowed the boys to use
when he didn't need it.

He rested it on his belly and settled in
comfortably before opening YouTube and
heading to his subscriptions.

Before clicking on the first video, however,
something else caught his eye.

From the bookshelf he saw different colored
pieces of construction paper hanging outwards,
jutted out towards him.

Moving the laptop to the side, he hoisted
himself up and walked over to the bookshelf.
He reached and pulled out the various colored

pages and ran his fingers over the nostalgic texture.

I haven't done anything with this stuff in a while.

He set the papers atop the shelf, reached farther back and pulled out a small pencil case. He opened it up to find markers, scissors, pencils. The essentials of course.

Gathering all his wayward supplies he took them to the kitchen and set them down on the kitchen table.

The feeling of being six years old again flooded back to him.

Nostalgia isn't just for the old after all.

What should I do with all this?

He counted up the pieces of construction paper, finding five of various colors.

I don't have too many. Can't mess this up and choose the wrong thing to draw. When's the last time I've done art anyways?

He thought it over and realized it had been more than a year ago.

Back when mom was still around.

He shook the sad thoughts out of his head and turned back towards his project.

He opened up the pencil case and rummaged inside before deciding to just empty it out on the table.

Running his hand over the markers, inspiration struck him.

I'll draw something for Sebastian and Jorge!

Although he wasn't entirely sure Sebastian deserved anything after he refused to take him out with him.

Nonetheless he got to work, suddenly filled to the brim with ideas.

Sebastian gets the green paper since that's his favorite color. Jorge gets red of course.

He paused before setting the purple paper aside for himself, his favorite color.

Sliding the green paper over, he began to sketch out an idea for Sebastian's picture, a small gray cat.

Once he was done drawing and coloring it, he set his portrait of Paz to the side and started on Jorge's drawing.

Wait a minute...what does Jorge like?

He looked around for something that could spark a memory in his head.

He likes music, I think. Wait, who doesn't like music?

He continued to think before it hit him.

Classic monster movies!

Before he knew it he had drawn out a perfect (in his 10 year old mind) picture of Frankenstein, The Wolf Man, Dracula, and, Jorge's favorite, Gill-Man.

He colored that one in and then set out to leave the pictures for his brothers to find.

Creaking open the door to Sebastian's room he walked in and set the picture down on his bed.

He wasn't usually allowed in Sebastian's room when he wasn't around.

He won't mind today, though. I come bearing gifts.

He giggled to himself, he had learned that phrase through a sitcom once, although he was drawing a blank on which one.

Before leaving Sebastian's room, as he passed by his nightstand, he noticed a note laying on it.

Curiosity getting the best of him, he picked it up and looked it over.

In flowery lettering it read:

I think of you all day

A small heart was drawn next to the single sentence. The paper was folded over many times, as if it was a note that had been passed around.

Oooooo. Sebastian's got a girlfriend.

Abel let out a laugh as he set the note back down and finally exited his brother's room.

Next he headed for Jorge's room, which was never off limits. He set down his monstrous picture and left quickly, nothing of interest in that room.

No love notes or anything, just the mostly empty room of an unemployed twenty one year old. Abel didn't notice that however, to him it was simply his older brother's room.

His <u>responsible</u> older brother's room.

The idea of Jorge keeping some kind of secret in there didn't even cross his mind. His brother was an honest man.

Back in the kitchen he sat down at the table once again, his purple sheet in front of him.

Time for something for me.

He knew just what to draw.

***

Jorge entered the house exhausted after a day of job hunting.

Oh good he's back!

Abel jumped up to greet his brother.

"How'd it go?"

Jorge shrugged. "I'm hoping good. It might be a little while before I hear back from anyone."

His oldest brother headed to the kitchen.

"What's there to eat?"

"Sebastian left some French toast from this morning for you."

"Ain't that nice of him." Jorge said. "Where is Seb anyways?"

"At Raul's again."

"Jeez that kid's parents must think we neglect him or something. He's there almost every day."

"I asked to go with him but he didn't let me." Abel complained, sitting from across his brother at the table.

"You know how he is. He's just a teenager right now, we're not cool enough for him."

Jorge chuckled and put the morning's French toast into the microwave. After a minute he pulled it out, grabbed a fork, and sat down with his youngest brother.

"So what'd you do today?"

"Not much." Abel answered. "Just some art."

Jorge nodded. "Nice. Nice. You'll have to show it to me eventually."

"Will do." Abel said, sliding over the purple piece of paper.

It was a drawing of the three brothers.

"Oh wow." Jorge said, picking it up in between bites. "This looks great, Abel."

Abel smiled with pride.

"In fact," Jorge said, standing up, "we're gonna put this right up on the fridge."

He grabbed a small strawberry magnet and placed it over the picture. "Looks great, little brother."

As he sat back down, Abel could feel butterflies of happiness in his stomach.

Just wait till you get to your room.

***

"Abel?" Sebastian shouted from his room. He walked down the hallway and into the living room. "Did you draw this?"

Abel nodded, happily.

Sebastian walked over and wrapped his arms around him and pulled him into a hug. "I love it little bro."

"That's not all." Jorge said from the couch. "Check this out."

He held up his monster picture. "Sick, ain't it?"

"You should see the fridge too." Abel said, standing to lead his brother over. "Look! It's us."

Sebastian held a corner of the drawing with his fingers and leaned in to look at it. "You're an amazing artist."

"Thank you, thank you." Abel said with a goofy intonation.

Sebastian walked off, staring at his picture while heading towards his room. Eventually Jorge also walked away, taking his.

Abel continued to stare at the image on the fridge, beaming with joy.

Jorge II

"Guess who went and got himself a job!" Jorge proclaimed as he hung up his phone. "This calls for a celebration!"

Sebastian and Abel ran up and hugged their brother, eventually knocking him down to the floor.

"Alright people, up! Up!" Jorge exclaimed from under the pile.

"Did you really finally get one?!" Abel shouted.

Gonna guess he meant that in a nicer way.

"Yup, next week I start at the Rent a Car by Wendy's. It's basically just a front desk job where I'm hooking people up with rides but I'll take what I can get."

The brothers stood up and dusted themselves off.

"Didn't I tell y'all to sweep up the floor a bit."

"Oh yeah," Sebastian said, "sorry about that I completely forgot."

Jorge pulled him in for a noogie. "No worries Seb."

"Ow! Ow!"

Sebastian pulled himself from his brother's grasp and rubbed the top of his head. "So I recall you mentioning something about a celebration?"

"I was thinking we could go out to eat. I'm kinda tired of fast food and frozen meals. Truthfully, I've been scared to spend money at a restaurant since the budget's been kinda tight. Now with the job I say we treat ourselves."

"Don't have to tell me twice." Sebastian said as he and Abel ran upstairs to get ready.

***

Okay maybe this is still not the best idea.

As they approached the Olive Garden, Jorge could feel a pit forming in his stomach.

The money he had been saving up was supposed to be in case of emergency and part of him felt like it still wasn't safe to spend.

It's okay to splurge every once in a while. Besides, the boys deserve to be treated.

But despite these reassurances he still couldn't shake the feeling.

I'll have steady money coming in soon enough. Enjoy the time with your brothers.

He parked and they all climbed out of the car and headed inside. They were promptly seated (*thank god we beat the lunchtime rush*) and began to look over the menu.

"You guys ready for school to start up again?"

The boys shook their head no as Jorge let out a laugh.

"We'll go get y'all's uniforms and supplies soon enough."

"I'm feeling a bit nervous about going back. Last year my teacher was awful, I feel like it'll just be a repeat." Abel said, turning over his kid's menu to the maze on the back.

"Yeah wait till you get to middle school." Sebastian assured him. "You'll have like 7 shitty teachers to chose from."

Jorge rolled his eyes. "That kind of cynicism really necessary?"

Sebastian shrugged. "You used to complain about your teachers all the time, why can't I?"

"That was different. My teachers were genuinely horrible."

"And mine aren't?"

"You never had a Ms. Wagner. Get one like her and you'll see what a *real* bad teacher is like."

"For your information," Sebastian said, matter of factly, "I did have Ms. Wagner! And may I remind you, *somebody* terrified me with stories about her the night before my first day of fifth grade!"

Oh yeah. I forgot about that.

"Well you got me there I suppose." Jorge smiled, turning back to look over the menu.

***

"Hey Sebastian!"

Jorge saw as his brother looked over towards a boy and his family being seated at a table nearby.

The boy waved as Sebastian smiled and waved back. Jorge took notice as the boy asked his parent something before he sprinted over towards the table.

The boy stood awkwardly for a moment before Sebastian introduced him.

"Uh, this is Raul. Y'know my friend I'm always mentioning."

So this is who's house he's always at.

"Hey there Raul, it's good to finally meet you. I'm Jorge, Seb's older brother."

"And I'm Abel. His little brother."

"Good to meet you all." Raul said. "Sebastian talks about you two all the time."

"Complaints, right?" Jorge said, extending his hand to offer a handshake to Raul.

Raul shook back. "Nah good things, always good things."

Raul looked over his shoulder back at his family. His mom, dad, and brother (who appeared close to Abel's age) were looking at their menus.

"I should probably get back to them." He said, waving bye. "It was good to meet you all though. You coming over today Sebastian?"

"I don't think so, maybe tomorrow."

"Oh okay, sounds good then."

"You're welcome to come over whenever you like, by the way." Jorge added.

"I'll have to take that offer up sometime." Raul said as he walked away.

Jorge looked over and made eye contact with Raul's father. Something about him seemed off. Angry.

He looked away and went back to his food.

***

Back in the car on the way home, Jorge decided it needed to be brought up.

"Hey Seb?"

"Yeah what's up?"

"Are Raul's parents nice to you?"

He shrugged a bit. "They're fine I guess. They don't really talk to me much or anything."

Guess I should just lay it all out.

"I've been thinking that maybe it'd be better for you not to go over so often, y'know?"

A confused look crossed Sebastian's face. "Why?"

"Well I mean they're a family, they need time to themselves and stuff. You're over there almost every day, they probably think you're neglected at home or something."

"It's not like that."

"Look they seem...alright I guess. Raul certainly seems like a good kid but his parents gave me some weird vibes. I caught his dad glaring at me."

"So?" Sebastian answered back defensively.

So? What's with the tone?

"Hey don't get angry with me or anything, I'm just telling you what I think."

"I think you're wrong."

Jorge gave him a serious look. "What's with the attitude?"

"I don't have an attitude."

"Spoken like someone with a bad fucking attitude."

The car was silent.

Sebastian was the first to break it. "I'm not gonna stop going."

"You will if I tell you to." Jorge snapped back. "I'm not telling you to stay away from your friend, just maybe back off from going to his house so much. Give his parents a break."

"So I'm a burden then, right? That's what you're trying to say."

Jorge sighed. "I didn't even say anything remotely close to that, Seb. Don't twist my words up like that, you know I can't stand when people put words in my mouth."

"I'm not putting words in your mouth, I'm clarifying your implications. Jerk."

"Look at you using big words." Jorge said, annoyed. "You call me a jerk when you're the one being one."

"You're the one acting like a parent. You're just my brother."

"Why are you saying shit like this, all cause I told you to stop bothering your friend's family? Why is this such a touchy subject for you?"

"Whatever." Sebastian said, turning his head away.

Jorge looked at the rear view mirror and saw Abel solemnly staring out the window. He looked like he wanted to cry.

What the hell is going on?

"Seb."

He continued to look away.

"Sebastian."

He turned his head slightly.

"I'm sorry if I upset you. I don't know why you're acting like this, but this isn't you. Whenever you wanna talk about it, I'm here."

Silence.

They reached home and everybody rushed inside to their respective rooms. Jorge flopped down on his bed, drained.

This isn't you Seb.

This isn't you.

Sebastian III

I think of you all day

Sebastian held the note in his hand, running his fingers over the carefully stenciled out heart below the short, but significant, sentence.

I think of you all day too.

He held the note to his chest and took a breath.

It was a weird feeling that he hadn't experienced before. To love someone romantically and to be loved back.

Or at least I think it's love.

What was love after all? He was only 13, he didn't really know. Was this it? These flutters in his stomach? The race in his heart?

Love.

He had loved people before, of course. Family mostly. But that was a different kind of love. This one was...special.

He folded the note back up and set it down on his nightstand.

The love note had proved sufficiently distracting for a few minutes but now he was back in reality. A reality where he was a complete jerk.

Why am I like this? Why do I put my brother through so much?

He felt twangs of guilt within him. It was rare for him to push Jorge like that. Sure he occasionally pushed his buttons, but that was in a funny way. This was something else.

This was mean.

He sighed and stood up from his bed. Making his way to his bedroom door, he wrapped his hand around the knob but stopped.

I want to apologize. Tell him how sorry I am.

So why didn't he?

Because I'm afraid.

In his heart he knew his brother wouldn't really be mad. Jorge was a lot of things and while temperamental was one of them, he didn't hold grudges and he wasn't hateful.

I know he loves me. So why am I so afraid to talk to him?

He let go of the knob and went back to his bed.

To say sorry?

Suddenly he heard a small **thwack** from his window.

Rushing over he looked out and saw Raul waving to him from the front lawn.

"Let's hang!" He mouthed, Sebastian barely able to read his lips.

He considered his options a moment, turning back to his door.

I really should apologize.

Then he turned back to Raul.

But maybe Jorge needs time anyways.

He opened his window and climbed out.

***

"Damn that sounds pretty shitty."

Sebastian nodded his head, taking strides to keep up with Raul.

"I know. I don't know why I'm such a jerk to him. He does so much for me and I treat him like that."

"You gonna apologize?"

Sebastian shrugged. "I mean, yeah of course. I just don't know when. Or what to say."

"Just be honest with him. He'll understand, I'm sure of it."

"How honest should I be?"

Raul took hold of Sebastian's hand. "As honest as you want to be. Tell him whatever you want."

Sebastian felt himself blush as his fingers intertwined with Raul's.

"I don't know. I'm still scared to tell him."

Raul nodded solemnly. "I get that. You were there when I told my parents...they weren't exactly happy."

Sebastian remembered alright. When Raul told his parents he was gay they lectured him about waiting till he was older to figure out what he was. Had it gone well, Raul planned to introduce Sebastian as his boyfriend, since it didn't however...

"Plus," Raul said, snapping Sebastian out of the memory, "I kinda think my dad knows about us."

"I wouldn't be surprised. I'm over almost everyday after all. I'm sure he could put 2 and 2 together. Also, Jorge said he saw your dad glaring at him."

"Yeah he can be kind of intimidating sometimes."

"Hey know what I was looking at earlier?"

"What?"

"The note you gave me. Y'know the one you passed me in class?"

Raul laughed. "Oh god that cheesy thing?"

Sebastian smiled. "It worked though. I mean we had been friends for awhile. I had been having those feelings but I thought it was just me."

"And I thought it was just me."

The boys smiled in silence thinking over the past.

When I'm with him I'm so happy.

They arrived at the local park and found a bench to sit at. With people around they let go of each other's hands. Back into friend mode.

"So have you thought over what to say?" Raul asked.

"I'm just gonna apologize for how I acted. But I don't think I'm ready to tell him <u>everything</u>."

"Yeah, I get that."

They got up and walked over to the monkey bars. Raul hoisted himself up to the top and then reached out to pull Sebastian up next.

It felt windier up top.

"Do you think Jorge suspects anything? Or your little brother...what was his name again?"

"Abel."

"Oh yeah, Abel. Do you think he does?"

"I doubt it. On both counts."

"You never know. I talked to my mom in private, she told me she always kinda knew. She still didn't think it was right though."

"She'll come around. She's pretty chill."

"Do you think your mom would've been okay with it?"

Sebastian thought it over.

"Honestly? I don't know."

"Well, regardless," Raul said, leaning his head on Sebastian's shoulder, "I think everything would've worked out."

***

When Sebastian got home that afternoon, he saw Jorge sitting at the kitchen table, looking over some papers.

No better time than now I suppose.

"Hey Jorge, can I talk to you?"

Jorge looked up from the papers. "Yeah of course."

Sebastian sat down and twiddled his thumbs awkwardly.

"I wanted to...apologize, I guess."

Jorge nodded.

"For earlier. I was being rude and shitty and I'm sorry. I ruined our day out."

Jorge stood and took the chair next to Sebastian. "Seb you didn't ruin anything. Tensions ran kinda high and I shouldn't have gotten so heated either. I'm sorry for losing my temper."

"It's okay. I'm sorry for pushing you to that point."

"Que sera sera."

Sebastian smiled and hugged his brother.

***

Back in his room he jumped onto his bed and rested his head against his pillows.

He reached over and opened up his note again.

Abel III

I'm so uncomfortable.

Abel attempted to fix his slightly too tight, baby blue collared shirt. It was the first day of school and now he was on the bus, winded and already done with the day.

The morning had been hectic, a rushed breakfast and a harried older brother attempting to get his siblings ready for the day set the stage for the pressuring mood.

Worst of all, as soon as they got to the bus stop Sebastian left to go with Raul on the middle school bus, leaving Abel all alone.

I wish we still rode the same one.

He knew it wasn't his brother's fault that he was going to a different school this year, but it still bothered him.

Resting his chin against his backpack which was crammed onto his lap, pressed against his belly, Abel thought over his intentions for this new school year.

It's gonna be the same as always. Boring.

He sighed before deciding to shift to a more positive headspace.

But I'm sure I can make it interesting.

He looked around the bus, in search of any of his friends but didn't spot a single one.

Despite the fact that his best friend Charlie had moved away early in the summer, he still always held out hope that he'd come back.

The first thing he did when he got on the bus was look for him.

Alas, there was no Charlie.

It's okay though. It's not like he was my only friend. When I get there everything will be alright.

***

The school hallways were crowded and noisy with the sound of elementary school kids, teachers welcoming them and concerned parents dropping them off.

He had found his name on the school door and the number to his room; 525.

Working his way there he finally saw a friendly face.

"Hey! Thomas!"

Thomas spun his head around and nodded towards Abel.

As Abel ran up to talk with him, he noticed Thomas kept facing forward, not turning to greet him.

"Hey man, what's up?" Abel said.

"Hey."

"What room are you in? I got 525."

"I don't know." He answered, coldly.

"Oh." Abel was taken aback by his demeanor. "Well they're up on the wall if you want to go see."

"Okay."

Abel walked beside him in silence as Thomas walked toward a printed sheet on the wall.

He expected Thomas to walk back to him and talk but instead Thomas kept on walking down the hall.

Determined, Abel ran to catch up with him.

"Hey so what room did you get?"

"523."

"Oh so we're close then. I was thinking that-"

"I gotta go man, bye."

"Oh. Okay."

Thomas walked off leaving Abel alone amongst the crowd.

Did I do something?

He thought back to the last time he had seen Thomas. Everything had been fine. In fact

Thomas had been one of the friendliest of their recess group.

But he was always closer to Charlie.

A worrying thought suddenly overcame him.

Maybe without Charlie people won't want to be around me.

He sulked his way to his classroom.

***

"In my classroom we obey the rules. No exceptions." Mr. Ramirez, Abel's new teacher, proclaimed.

"We are silent when we need to be. We don't talk outside of what is necessary. When you have work to turn in you <u>will</u> turn it in to the designated homework tray on my desk. If it is a daily assignment it <u>will</u> go into the other tray. Is that clear?"

"Yes." Half the classroom answered, unenthusiastically.

"I said, Is that clear?"

"Yes." Now it was the whole class.

"Good. Today we'll be doing a small writing assignment. I want to know all about you."

Abel opened up his red spiral journal and unzipped his pencil bag.

He pondered what he should say.

"Have it be at least a paragraph long. Tell me some of the things you do for fun, about your parents, siblings, friends, anything. I just want to know about *you*."

Abel began to write.

My name is Abel Gonzalez. I am 10 years old. I live with my two older brothers, Jorge and Sebastian. My mom passed away last year and that is why I live with my brothers. I don't know where my dad is. My best friend is Charlie but he moved away.

He looked over the paragraph and realized that there really wasn't much to him.

This looks kinda sad.

Even seeing the word mom written out nearly put a lump in his throat.

Oh well. I guess it's the truth after all.

He continued.

I like to draw and watch YouTube. When I grow up I want to help people. My favorite book is Bunnicula.

And...that was it.

Is this enough? I can't think of what else to write.

He set his pencil down and looked around. Everybody else was still writing.

He tapped his fingers against the desk's surface and realized that everything today was just making him sad.

He didn't like being sad and always tried to see the good in things. Today was testing him, however.

A few minutes passed before it was time to share.

Mr. Ramirez went down the line and had people read out their writings. Some kids took long, others not so much.

When it was Abel's turn, he stood and meekly read out his paragraph.

It made him nervous to have all eyes on him but he read as quickly as he could before sitting back down.

He felt like crying.

Next to him, a girl with shiny blonde hair leaned over.

"I'm sorry about your mom." She whispered.

"Oh, thanks." Abel said sheepishly before lowering his eyes.

The girl turned back away from him.

He never liked the pity that came along with having a deceased parent. Everybody told him they were sorry, but what were they sorry for?

There's nothing they could've done.

Don't be rude. People are just trying to be nice.

But sometimes the unneeded niceness bothered him. He didn't like people talking about his mom. It was his cross to bear.

I shouldn't have brought her up. Now everybody feels bad for me.

He huffed out his nose and tried to pay attention to the people reading.

Everybody felt bad for him and he felt bad for himself.

Jorge III

Jorge sat in his car, head against the steering wheel, crying.

His first day at his new job had gone absolutely terrible.

Terrible customers, terrible boss, terrible coworkers. Just...terrible.

I can't catch a break. I can't catch a fucking break.

He felt a pain in the middle of his stomach. Pressing his hand to it, he grit his teeth.

The stress is gonna kill me.

A micromanaging boss, disrespectful customers, mean coworkers. This was his new life now, day in and day out.

Putting up with all this for money. Money makes the world go round after all.

He wiped the tears from his eyes and looked at himself in the mirror.

Get ahold of yourself. How many times are you gonna sit here crying in your car?

"Yeah." He told himself. "No more."

He pulled out of the parking lot and sped off.

***

"Give me the biggest burger you have." He announced into the speaker.

"That'd be the Bacon Triple Stack, you good with that?"

"Sounds good to me."

"To drink?"

"A large Dr. Pepper."

"I'll have your total for you at the first window."

He pulled up, got his order and drove off to find a spot to park.

Finding a nice shaded area, he exited his car and sat underneath a tree, something he hadn't done in forever.

He took a deep breath and let the soft wind brush past him.

When's the last time you've taken a moment like this?

He closed his eyes and leaned his head against the tree.

Since mom.

He remembered it like it was yesterday. Whenever he had a bad day at school, a shitty shitty day, she'd drive him out to a nice spot and they'd share a meal. All while basking under the beautiful tree shade.

"Life's tough, mijo." He remembered her saying. "It's so tough that sometimes I just feel like disappearing. Todos los dias, trabajando, cuidando a ustedes. It's hard."

"How do you get through it?"

His mother paused for a moment.

"You just do."

He remembered thinking it over while they ate.

"The kids at school don't like me." He finally told her. "They treat me like I'm annoying. Everything I do bothers them."

His mother ran her hand through his hair. "They just don't know how great you really are."

"I'm not great, Mom. I'm nothing. I just wish I could fade away."

Wrapping her arm around him, she pulled him in close.

"You can't just fade away. Life's tough now but things change. You stick around and you'll be happy you did. Trust me."

He remembers leaning into her. He could hear her heartbeat in his ear.

"Besides," she said, "what would your brothers do without you?"

In the present, Jorge opened his eyes.

"What would your brothers do without you?"

Goddamn Mom, you didn't know it at the time but that sentence is so important. All these bad days, everything I go through...you had to go through it too. You did it for us, now I have to do it for them.

It was a cycle, one that was supposed to be broken. But when his mom died it just started all over.

"Mom." Jorge spoke into the air. "I miss you."

The air picked up and he finally unwrapped his burger and took the biggest bite he could.

I feel trapped, like there's no end to what I have to deal with. But now thinking it over, I'm sure that's how she felt too.

He thought back to another day when he found her crying in the kitchen. She was there, sitting in front of a mountain of bills. It was after midnight.

"Mom?" He had asked.

She lifted her head up and quickly wiped her tears.

"Hey baby you scared me. Why're you up? You have school tomorrow, remember?"

"Actually I don't. We have an unused snow day so we get a day off. What's happening?"

"It's all these bills. I don't think I have enough money to pay them all. I think we're gonna have to cut the cable."

"Oh." He remember saying as he sat down at the table. "Well, that's okay. There's never anything good on anyways. Puro basura, right?"

She laughed. "Yeah, I suppose."

"Also now that Abel is almost potty trained we can stop buying diapers and that'll help too."

"Thank god for that. Dirty diapers are no fun."

"See? It'll all work out."

She nodded. "I know. It's just so hard to deal with it all. Sometimes I feel like I'm being suffocated by life. Like I can't breathe."

Jorge sat in silence.

Listening.

It was what she needed most.

"These days go on and on. I feel like I can't catch a break."

She looked up at him. "But you boys make life worth living."

She walked over to hug him. "I love you mijo."

"Love you too, Mom." Jorge answered back. "When I'm older I'm gonna work hard and make enough money so that you never have to work again."

He remembered the warm smile that spread across her face. "That's nice, but you should live your life. You shouldn't have to live it to support me. I want you to have your own life."

The memory snapped him back to reality.

My own life? I definitely don't have that now.

He sighed and finished up his burger. Lately the memories of his mother had been building. He missed her so bad, but also, he missed when she was alive and he could have his own life.

It felt selfish to think. His brother's needed him and he'd sacrifice his life and time for them.

But he missed the life he used to have.

Hanging out with friends, going to parties, making out with girls.

His high school years had been wild and a definite improvement over elementary school, where he was more of an outcast.

Throughout middle school, he reinvented himself. Became the person he wanted to be. And, all through high school, he was that person.

And then there was Bea too...

He shook his head and cleared his mind. He didn't want to think about old flames.

A year out from his mother's death he had slipped back into being nothing.

Being someone who wanted to fade away.

You can't just fade away.

His mother's words echoed in his head as he got up, tossed his trash in a garbage bin and walked back to his car.

He drove off in silence.

Sebastian IV

Sebastian slowly slid the heavy wooden pallet over.

Behind it, a hole just big enough to shimmy through gave him an entrance into the abandoned office building.

He climbed in, brushing the dust and cob webs off himself, then began to look around.

As dangerous as it was to be somewhere like this, it was nothing new for Sebastian. He had been coming here for almost a year.

I know I left it here somewhere.

He rummaged through a metallic, broken down desk, checking each cabinet for what he was looking for.

There it is.

He lifted up the big, metal flash light and clicked it on.

It lit up the darkness around him and he took off, walking deeper into the building.

The suffocating dark was almost comforting to him, just like it had been a little under a year ago when he discovered this place. After a particularly nasty fight with Jorge he ran off, looking for somewhere to be alone.

And to think I knocked over that pallet by accident.

Once inside he remembered crying on the bottom floor, upset. Upset at his brother, upset at his recently deceased mother, upset at her last days.

After letting all his emotions out in the surrounding dark he immediately felt much better. He returned home and made things right again.

By the next time he was there he began exploring the building, now equipped with the flash light.

He never really understood why this place was so appealing to him.

I know places like this can be dangerous, but a little danger never hurt nobody. Well actually that's not true but still.

He only ever came alone, he never even mentioned this place to anybody. While he definitely had considered telling his brothers or Raul about this place, he never went through with it.

They wouldn't understand.

This was a place of his own. Just for him and no one else.

A place to think and calm himself down when things got tough. Or sometimes just a place to relax. The darkness enveloping him and taking his worries away.

As he made his way up the stairs, illuminating in front of himself and taking his time, he suddenly felt a slight give as he stepped onto the 2nd floor.

Huh. That doesn't usually happen.

He continued to step forward, walking casually over to the stack of books he sometimes liked to flip through when suddenly the floor gave out.

He yelped as he tumbled downwards, landing hard on his back. Now he was back on the bottom floor.

In a daze, he moved his hands around the darkness attempting to find his flashlight.

Ow. I'm an idiot.

Feeling a warmness around his head he reached up and felt a stickiness matted against his hair.

I'm bleeding!

He felt panic begin to set in as he tried to sit up, before the pain caused him to lay back down. Rolling himself over, he ended up on his stomach, hands brushing against the ground.

His fingers brushed against a metallic cold as he finally wrapped his hands around the flashlight.

Attempting to click it on, he realized that it had broken in the fall.

The darkness didn't feel comforting anymore, it felt terrifying.

He bent his knees forcing himself up a bit as he shifted his weight onto them.

Taking a moment to breathe, he touched the back of his head again. It was even wetter than before.

I can't believe I'm stuck here bleeding in the dark.

He tried to force himself up again but the pain in his back knocked him back down.

C'mon Sebastian, get up!

He lowered his head and reached into his pocket. He had to do something he hated doing.

He had to call Jorge and ask for help.

Of course when he pulled his phone out, it was dead.

Great. Thanks Abel, glad you charged it when you finished playing on it. Oh well, this garbage phone never really works without wifi anyways. Doubt there's any in here.

He stuffed his phone in his pocket again and reached out until he felt the edge of a desk.

The dust of it now mixing with the blood on his fingertips, he used it to steady himself and stand up.

A scream of pain escaped him as he straightened himself out, finally up on his feet.

He slowly began to shamble towards the exit.

***

Finally back in the light he could see the damage he had caused.

His fingers were caked in a dark red color, a sick blend of blood, dust and dirt.

He looked down to see his once blue basketball shorts filthy and chalky. Same for his tee which looked like it was covered in an unrecognizable pattern.

He began to walk home, slowly forcing himself despite the pains in his head and back and, opening the front door, he was greeted by his brother's stares.

"Holy shit, Seb! What happened to you?" Jorge said, running over to his injured brother.

"I fell."

"Fell?! Fell where?"

"I was out exploring, y'know like I usually do and I took a tumble on my way down."

A slight lie. Better to think of it as a half truth.

"Is that blood?" Abel asked, holding up his brother's hand.

"Yeah, I hit my head when I landed."

"Here let me see."

Jorge maneuvered around him and began to check his head.

"Jesus Seb how do you get yourself into these situations?!"

"Is it bad?"

"I see a scrape but not really an opening or anything. That's a lot of blood though so we're gonna have to take you to the hospital."

"No! C'mon Jorge it's not that bad. I'm fine, really."

"Fine? You can barely even stand, you look like you're gonna collapse at any moment!"

Sebastian huffed, knowing that he wasn't gonna be able to talk himself out of a hospital visit.

"Let's just go."

Wrapping his arm around Jorge and being steadied by Abel, Sebastian began to make his way to the car.

His back pained, a smile still managed to cross his face.

How do I get myself into these situations?

Jorge IV

"Honestly Seb, it's a miracle I somehow manage to keep y'all alive." Jorge said, lowering his face into his palms.

Sat in the stark white hospital room, the three brothers began to laugh.

Though their arrival there had been mostly stressful and worrisome, by now it was something else. Something lighter.

It feels good to laugh.

"I still don't understand what you were even doing in there." Abel said as the laughter died down.

"Yeah," Jorge added, "you couldn't have picked some place a little less dangerous? An abandoned office building is like on the top ten of bad places I can think of."

Sebastian smiled. "I don't really know what I was thinking. I guess I just liked the way that place felt, y'know?"

Jorge and Abel looked at each other.

"Nah I don't know."

"Yeah sorry bro I don't really get it."

It was silent for a beat before the laughter started again.

"Also," Abel interjected, "no lie, you look ridiculous with that bandage on your head."

It was true. Sebastian, despite being beaten up by his fall, looked absolutely silly with his head wrapped up in the scratchy gauze. It wasn't even a big cut.

Gonna be a big hospital bill though.

The thought of payment briefly worried Jorge, but looking at his brothers made the negativity slowly seep out from his mind.

Who cares about money right now? I'll worry later. All I do is worry, worry, worry. Maybe it's good to take a step back sometimes and chill out. Look at the boys, they're happy.

And mostly healthy.

"Ugh I really do think they went a little over board with all this." Sebastian said, rubbing his wrapped head. "I felt a lot better by the time we got here. You'd think I'd been shot in the head or something."

"Probably mostly a formality thing." Jorge said. "Stop moving it."

"I can't! It's so itchy."

"Let me feel." Abel said, reaching over to lightly pet his brother's head.

"Oh yeah I'd go crazy with that on me."

"When's the last time we've even been in a hospital?" Jorge asked.

The brothers took a moment to think it over.

"Oh yeah." Abel finally said. "Remember a couple months ago when Sebastian twisted his ankle pretty bad?"

Sebastian rolled his eyes. "I'm starting to think it's always my fault we're here."

"We were here a lot for Mom too."

"Yeah but that's different."

"How so?" Jorge questioned.

"Because that was under sad circumstances." Sebastian answered. "The times we're here with me are funny."

"No they're boring." Abel said. "We're always stuck here for hours with nothing to do."

"Not true. You spend most of your time here begging me for some money for the vending machine."

Abel took a bite of his Honey Bun. "I have no idea what you're talking about."

Jorge rustled his hair, playfully. "Honestly being in a hospital always makes me think of Mom. Even if we're here for funny reasons. These rooms just take me back."

"I can see that." Sebastian sympathized. "But at the same time, I always hope the new memories will overtake those old ones."

"I don't want to lose any memories I have of Mom." Jorge said.

"Yeah me neither." Abel agreed.

"I'm not saying I want them to disappear." Sebastian said, defending himself. "I just don't want my life to be spent thinking about all the sad shit that's happened."

"Okay actually I agree with that more." Abel said.

Jorge nodded his head. "I guess I'm just scared to move on in some ways. I know I jokingly said I don't understand why you liked that building, but that's not true. You know Alamo Park, near the Walmart?"

Sebastian and Abel nodded.

"I go there sometimes to clear my head. Kinda like how you would go to that building to clear yours. I go there and I think about Mom a lot. Way more than I do normally. It's like I have to remind myself of her. I don't want to forget."

"When I would go to the building, I'd think about her too. Sometimes though, I would go and avoid thinking about her. I get too sad when she's the focus of my thoughts. Is that bad?"

Abel climbed onto the hospital bed and rested his head on Sebastian's shoulder. "I don't think it is."

"What about you, Abel?" Jorge questioned. "When do you think about her?"

"All the time. I get scared though because sometimes I can't really remember her voice."

"I have that problem too." Sebastian said.

"Me too."

The boys took a moment.

When's the last time we've talked about Mom like this? Other than on the anniversary of her death, of course. We usually only bring her up in passing but I don't think the three of us talk like this often.

Maybe we should do it more.

"Her Facebook page is still up." Jorge said, breaking the silence. "I'll show y'all how to get on it when we get home. She has tons of videos on there with her voice. Sometimes I log on to hear her again."

"I'd like that." Abel said, softly.

I don't know why I hadn't told them this before. I mean I guess I thought I was the only one that had trouble remembering Mom's voice. It made me feel so shitty, but now knowing they struggle with it too... I don't feel so bad anymore.

"Hey Jorge?" Sebastian said, shaking his older brother from his thoughts.

"Yeah what's up?"

"Can *I* have money for the vending machine?"

Jorge laughed. "Now you too? Of course you can, Seb."

He reached into his pocket before pulling out 3 crinkled up bills.

"Here, tell Abel what you want and he can go get it for you. They'd probably get mad if you were up and about."

Jorge handed Abel the dollars as he slipped back into his thoughts.

If I had the money I'd for sure put it towards some family therapy. I feel like it'd be good for us to have a healthy outlet for letting our feelings out. Something to help us talk things through.

If I had the money, of course.

For now Jorge had to be content with the fact that they all had each other. They could rely on each other, talk to each other, be open.

And sometimes that's the best that you can hope for.

Abel IV

I hate being in the cafeteria.

Despite his love of food, Abel never felt comfortable in the school lunchroom.

Always alone and feeling awkward, this school year was really testing his resolve.

I feel like I don't know how to act when I'm sitting alone. I look at everybody else, talking with their friends, having fun and I don't know how **I** *should act.*

Do I come off unfriendly? Is it hard to walk up to me and talk? Am I scary?

He opened up his journal to a fresh page and began to doodle. His favorite thing to do was start drawing with nothing in mind. Just putting pencil to paper and seeing where it took him.

The problem, this time, was that it was taking him nowhere.

An...animal? Monster, maybe? Or wait, maybe a car.

He continued to fill the page but the uncomfortableness of the situation surrounding him seemed insurmountable.

Not even drawing proved a fitting distraction.

He laid his pencil down and closed the journal.

I give up.

Stuffing his items back into his clear plastic backpack, he pulled out his lunchbox and removed the PB&J sandwich Jorge had made for him.

My stomach's upset.

The past couple of days had left him feeling anxious and it was starting to cause even meals to be difficult.

Just eat. Forget about where you are and eat.

He began to take small bites, when suddenly he felt a soft tap on his shoulder.

Turning around, he locked eyes with the pale blonde girl who had wished him condolences on the first day of school.

"Sorry to bother," she said, "but I don't really have anywhere to sit and I'm tired of eating in the hallway. Is it okay to sit with you?"

Abel froze for a moment, mostly in confusion, before answering.

"Uh yeah, of course." He said, scooting over as he did. "Here let me make room."

She took the seat beside him and unlatched her tin lunchbox.

"Ugh my mom packed a salad again today. She promised me when this school year started she's switch it up more than last year. Guess not."

"My brother pretty much packs me a sandwich everyday." Abel said, holding up his PB&J. "I don't really mind that much cause it's my favorite. Still, it does get a little boring."

"Tell me about it." She said, emptying a small packet of ranch into the bowl before mixing it up with a fork. "My name is Sidney by the way."

"I'm Abel."

"Abel! That's what it was. I know we did those introductions in class but I kinda zoned out a little."

"Yeah me too."

He said this though in reality he had remembered her name. His memory was a speciality of his, but in the interest of not coming off like a freak, he kept it to himself.

"So are you new to this school too?" She asked.

"Oh, no. My best friend moved away over the summer and I've been kinda stuck on my own since then."

"Sorry I shouldn't have assumed anything. I'm new here we moved over the summer. I miss my old school and my old friends."

"I'm sure you do. I know how much it sucks to miss people."

"Yeah it really does. I thought I'd adjust okay but my plan hasn't really worked out."

"You mentioned eating alone in the hallways."

She let out a small laugh. "Yeah I felt like such a loser. When I came in today I was determined to sit with people."

"What made you choose me?"

She shrugged. "You seemed nice, plus we had a class together. Also I remembered you mentioning that your mom passed away and I could relate to that. Not my mom, but my dad passed away a year and a half ago."

"Oh I'm really sorry to hear that."

"It's fine, I mean I'm pretty much past it. For the most part."

"Yeah I'm like that with my mom. Sorta."

It grew quiet for a bit as the two ate their lunches.

I don't know if it's weird to talk about dead parents as a first conversation, but I'm happy to have someone to eat with.

It wasn't long before the bell rang to go back to class.

"That felt fast." She said, packing up her things. "But it was nice having someone to eat with. Is it okay for me to sit here again tomorrow?"

79

"Yeah, definitely." Abel answered, attempting to hide his enthusiasm.

"Sounds good!" Sidney said as she turned away with a smile.

***

That day Abel smiled the whole school bus ride home.

She was so nice. And having someone to eat with...that was awesome. No more awkward lunches alone.

Looking out the window at the passing blur of trees he found himself still thinking of her.

He kept replaying the interactions in his head, how good it felt to be friendly with someone again.

It's weird but I just feel so happy to have a friend. I don't like like her or anything like that. She just seems so cool and nice. It's like I'm excited to finally have someone to talk to at school.

As he hopped off the bus and ran towards his house, the excitement continued. He needed to talk to someone.

Whenever Abel was happy he liked the whole world to know.

He ran into the house and straight to Sebastian's room.

Barging in, ready to share the good news, he stepped inside.

"Sebastian! I made a-"

He stopped suddenly as Sebastian and Raul quickly pulled their faces from one another.

"Abel! You're supposed to knock!" Sebastian shouted.

"S-sorry." Abel managed to squeak out as he slammed the door shut.

He felt himself shaking as he slid down against the wall, before then running to his own room.

He sat on his bed, still stunned from the interaction.

Were Sebastian and Raul...kissing?

Suddenly the butterflies of happiness in his stomach felt more like nerves.

He felt like he walked in on something secretive. Not bad necessarily but something he shouldn't have known.

Sebastian is gonna be so pissed.

Sebastian V

I am so pissed.

Sebastian paced around his room, chewing on the edge of his nail.

I always tell him to knock! How hard is it to remember that?!

I can't believe it. The first time Raul comes over to my house and this is what happens. Why wasn't I more careful? I should've locked the door or-

"Sebastian?"

Sebastian looked up as Raul's voice knocked him from his dizzying thoughts.

"You ok?" Raul asked, motioning for him to sit beside him.

With an exasperated sigh, Sebastian sat on the bed and lowered his face into his hands.

"Yeah I'm okay. I just don't really know how to feel right now."

"Do you think he'll tell your brother? Your older one, that is."

"I don't really know. I don't know what's going on, what he's thinking, what he's gonna say. Plus Abel is the absolute worst at keeping secrets. I don't think this is gonna stay hidden for long."

Raul sat pensively before placing his hand on Sebastian's shoulder. "Maybe this is a blessing in disguise?"

That made Sebastian chuckle. "I wish. Part of me highly doubts that though."

"Why?"

"Hmm?"

"Why do you doubt that? You always tell me how close you are to your brothers. Why do you worry about what they'll say to you?"

"It's complicated."

"Lay it on me."

"I don't know, I figure they'll accept me but I just don't feel ready for them to know. Or at least I didn't. Cat's out of the bag, I suppose."

"Not completely."

"What do you mean by that?"

"Abel hasn't told anyone yet." Raul said, leaning against Sebastian's arm. "You could talk to him and work things out."

"I want to." Sebastian said, apprehensively. "I want everything to be ok and to work out. But this is **NOT** how I expected things to go."

"What were you expecting?"

"Something...calm. Normal and chill. I'd come out to them and everything would be the same. I never wanted to make a big show about coming out. But this? This is straight out of a sitcom."

"Things might've started out a little crazy but that doesn't mean it has to stay that way. You work things out with Abel right now and then maybe you'll still get your low key coming out with Jorge."

Sebastian nodded. "Can I be honest?"

"Of course."

"I'm scared to even talk to Abel. He looked shell shocked when he barged in. I'm worried that he's already seeing me differently."

"Well," Raul said, standing, "only one way to find out."

***

The walk to Abel's room felt endless.

C'mon Sebastian. Just go in there and talk to him.

Gently, he knocked on Abel's door. Turning behind him, he saw Raul, from his bedroom doorway, flash him a thumbs up.

Just as he was about to knock again, Abel spoke.

"Come in."

With a deep breath, Sebastian reached for the handle and twisted it, entering his little brother's room.

Abel was on his bed, cradling a pillow and sheepishly avoiding eye contact with Sebastian.

"Uh hey," Sebastian said, awkwardly, "I was hoping we could talk."

"Okay."

Sebastian took a seat next to him.

"I actually don't know where to begin really. I guess I should just be upfront. I'm, y'know..."

Abel turned to look at him, waiting for him to continue.

"Well, um, I'm like..." Sebastian stuttered out.

Sighing he decided to just get it out. "I'm gay, okay?"

Abel nodded his head and buried his chin into his pillow. "I figured."

Sebastian let out a small laugh. "I still feel a little uncomfortable being open I guess. Nobody knows other than Raul and well, you now I suppose. This really isn't how I wanted to do this. At all."

"I won't tell anybody."

"Thanks, really. Are you ok though?"

Abel shrugged. "Yeah I was just really surprised. And truthfully, I felt bad."

"Bad? Why?"

"Cause you always tell me to knock and I never listen and now I messed up and exposed you."

"It's okay."

"Are you mad at me?"

Sebastian smiled. "Nah it's all good. And just to be clear, please don't tell Jorge. I want to when I'm good and ready."

"Can I ask why you don't want him to know?"

"It's nothing against Jorge, I know he loves us. He's just always so busy and his schedule is so erratic and hectic and I don't want to add more trouble to his life. I don't want to burden him with my problems."

"He doesn't think of us as burdens."

"No, I know. But I just feel like right now isn't a good time. I want things to stabilize first."

"And Raul..."

"Yeah, Raul's my boyfriend."

"Since when?"

"It's been a little while now. He's really nice."

"So that love note was from him?"

"Wait," Sebastian said, puzzled, "how do you know about the note?"

"Oh." Abel said, catching his slip up. "I kinda sorta read it when I left my drawing for you in your room."

Sebastian rolled his eyes. "Kinda, sorta, eh?"

Abel smiled mischievously.

"I do have something I need to ask." Sebastian said, growing serious.

"What?"

"Does finding this out about me, change how you see me?"

Abel shook his head. "Not at all."

"You still love me the same as before?"

"You know I do."

The brothers embraced into a great big bear hug.

"Thank you, Abel. If someone had to find out first, I'm glad it was you."

"No problem bro."

They pulled away from each other and sat on the bed quietly.

"What was it that you barged into my room for, anyways?" Sebastian asked.

"Oh yeah. I finally made a friend at school! Her name's Sidney, she's really nice."

"I'm happy to hear that. How'd y'all meet?"

"I was sitting by myself at lunch and she joined me. She said she didn't have anyone to sit with either."

"I'm glad you two could find each other then."

Sebastian stood from the bed.

"Would you like to properly meet Raul? Now not just as my friend, but as my boyfriend?"

"Sounds good." Abel said with a smile.

Sebastian walked Abel to his room, where Raul sat patiently on the bed.

"Raul, I'd like you to meet my awesome little brother, Abel. I know y'all technically met at the restaurant, but I'd say circumstances are pretty different now." Sebastian said.

Raul laughed and extended his hand outward. "It's good to meet you little dude."

Abel smiled and shook his hand back. "Good to meet you too."

***

"Well it's been a pretty exciting day." Raul said, nearly out the front door. "I should get home though, before my parents start freaking out."

"It was nice talking to you!" Abel shouted from the couch.

"Same to you!"

Raul turned towards Sebastian.

"Today didn't really go the way you wanted, but for what it's worth I had an awesome time."

Sebastian blushed. "You're welcome back anytime you want."

Raul planted a soft kiss on Sebastian's cheek and quietly left, shutting the door behind him.

"I like him." Abel said happily.

Me too.

Jorge V

It had been a long, long day.

Jorge climbed into his car, feet aching from work and ready to head home.

I'm finally done.

Cracking his knuckles and starting up the car he decided to check his phone before pulling away.

I should see if the boys needed anything.

They didn't have their own cellphones but they had access to Jorge's old ones. No service, which means they basically only work when connected to WiFi. Still he was able to call them through Snapchat and Messenger.

He clicked his phone open and froze.

On his home screen was a message he wasn't expecting. An unknown number, but the text under it shocked him.

Jorge this is your dad. I'd like to talk with you.

His fingertips went numb as his breath quickened. He threw his phone to the seat beside him and shoved open his door.

Collapsing to the ground and vomiting, the words kept repeating in his mind.

This is your dad. Your dad.

"FUCK!!!" He shouted, wiping his mouth with his hoodie sleeve.

He banged his fist on the side of his car and got back in.

No. Not dad.

He gripped the steering wheel, released, gripped again. Over and over.

How did he get my number? What the hell do I do?

Suddenly everything was rising back up. The abandonment issues, the verbal abuse, the anger.

It was all coming back.

Abel and Sebastian didn't know. They didn't remember. How could they? They were 1 and 4 when he left.

Jorge, however, was 12 and he remembered everything.

His father had his moments. Sometimes he was nice and playful but when he was drunk he was a mean, awful man.

Worst of all was how he treated his wife.

Whore. Slut. Puta. All the words he used to call Mom.

He took notice of how his hands were still shaking, clamped onto the steering wheel. He didn't know if it was from fear, anxiety, or anger.

Maybe all three.

Nine years. Gone for nine years and he decides to show up out of the blue and mess everything up again.

"Why can't you just stay away?!!!" Jorge shouted.

He slammed his forehead against the steering wheel and began to sob.

The trauma that he put away nine years ago was here again.

You were gone! You left and we moved on!

Had he though? He was starting to question if he truly had moved on. Obviously it was all buried down deep, hidden.

The worst part was the conflict inside of him. He had been simultaneously dealing with his father's abandonment and also the joy that his abuser was gone. It left him conflicted within.

Now every emotion was beating down on him, taking him back to the terrified 12 year old who didn't know what lay ahead.

I can't tell the boys. I'm gonna ignore that message and move on with my life. I spent 9 years forgetting. I'm not gonna let it all come back.

Still shaking he turned the car on and pulled out of the parking lot.

I don't feel like driving, but I have to get home. I need to get out of this damn parking lot.

It was decided. He'd bury that message in the recesses of his mind just like he had buried everything else having to do with his father.

I'm changing things. I'm gonna save up money and move us out of this town. Start over completely and leave it all behind.

We need a fresh start.

He was still shaking when he made it to the house.

He looked at the time on his phone.

11:36.

He took a moment to clear his messages before heading in.

The house was silent. He checked on the boys to see that each was asleep in their rooms.

They lay there, peaceful.

Jorge smiled as tears streamed down his cheeks.

He looked at Abel, just as innocent as 9 years ago. He didn't know what was happening then, and he wouldn't now.

This is my cross to bear.

And Sebastian, the Tasmanian Devil of the family. Though he had been 4 he had never understood the magnitude of their father's cruelty. Jorge shielded him from everything.

I protected you from him, Seb. And I still will. I promise.

He wiped his tears and headed for his room. Getting into bed he realized that the shaking hadn't stopped.

God my adrenaline is going crazy. One text managed to ruin my whole night.

He lay in bed, staring up at the ceiling. The memories continued to flow, overtaking his thoughts and filling his mind.

"C'mon Seb, let's go play in the other room."
"Don't listen to the yelling, they're just working things out."
"Help me with Abel, he won't stop crying with all the noise."
"Go to sleep, Seb. They'll stop fighting soon. Everything is okay."

All the things he used to say to shield his brothers. All the half truths and lies to preserve their innocence.

I'll do everything in my power to keep him out and away. With mom gone it's my responsibility to save them from him.

I don't care if he's changed or is a born again Christian now or whatever bullshit he'll try to peddle. People never really change. Who's to say that he won't go back to his old ways as soon as we're in his grasp.

No. He's not getting anywhere near us.

He's gonna go back to not existing for me. He's gonna be a ghost again.

I'm moving on.

The scariest part though? No matter how much Jorge repeated it to himself, he doubted that he'd ever fully move on.

It felt like his father's shadow would always be over him. Within him.

Haunting him.

There's no moving on for children of trauma. There's no forgetting or getting better. No matter how deep the pain is buried it will live on in my mind. It will be there.

Always.

Jorge didn't sleep that night.

Abel V

"Is it a Gone Day?" Abel asked as Sebastian exited Jorge's room.

"Looks like it. I mean usually he'll at least murmur something out but whatever's wrong today must be big. He didn't say anything at all."

A concerned look crossed Abel's face.

What could've happened?

"He got home pretty late last night." Sebastian said, beginning to walk towards the kitchen. "Maybe something bad happened at work."

"Do you think they fired him? Today's Saturday, he works on Saturdays."

"Maybe. Would explain why he didn't get up to go." Sebastian said with a sigh.

Abel sat at the kitchen table and rested his forehead against the top.

Poor Jorge. I hope he still has his job.

"Should we go in and take him some breakfast?" Abel asked.

"I don't know. Usually we just leave food here for when he decides to come out."

"I know, but maybe we should try something different."

"A new approach?"

"Worth a shot. I don't like just leaving him in there alone."

"Okay." Sebastian said, determined. "Let's try."

***

The boys creaked open the door to Jorge's room, slowly entering with a plate of eggs and bacon.

Abel looked at the mass underneath the bedsheets. He felt a knot in his stomach.

This feels like something from a scary movie.

Sebastian was usually the one who handled Jorge on his Gone Days. Abel mostly waited outside, often not seeing Jorge until he dragged himself out of the room.

"Hey, Jorge?" Sebastian said softly.

The mass remained still.

"We got you some breakfast. Abel's here too."

Still nothing.

The boys began to approach the bed. Sebastian set the breakfast down on the nightstand.

"J-Jorge?" Abel muttered out.

Finally the mass began to move.

"I'm okay. Y'all don't have to worry about me." Jorge croaked out.

Abel felt a tinge of frustration.

How could we not worry about you? Somethings wrong and you're barely speaking.

"C'mon Abel, let's give him some space."

Sebastian tugged at his little brother's arm but Abel pulled away.

"No." Abel said.

"No?"

"No. I'm not leaving until Jorge tells us what's wrong."

They both looked over at their older brother who still didn't move.

"It's nothing Abel."

"No it's not nothing, Jorge. You have your Gone Days and they scare me. You never tell us what's wrong or what's behind them and that makes me worry. We love you. Let us help you."

Finally Jorge turned to look at them.

"I'm sorry." He said, fixing himself and sitting up. "I don't do this for attention or to worry you. Sometimes things happen in my life that just stop me dead in my tracks. I can't always participate."

"Participate in what?" Sebastian asked.

"In life." Jorge responded. "I can usually force myself to keep going but there are times where that's just not possible."

"But what happened this time?" Abel said, climbing onto the bed. Sebastian followed.

Jorge looked at them with red, tired eyes. He thought for a moment before shaking his head.

"I don't want to say."

C'mon Jorge.

"You can tell us. Whatever it is." Abel said, moving closer to Jorge.

"We promise we'll help you." Sebastian added.

Jorge sighed and rubbed his eyes. "Okay. But before I tell you I'm gonna ask that you make a promise to me."

The boys nodded.

"Promise me that no matter what I say, we'll move on from it. That we won't...focus our lives around this. Promise me you won't go digging deeper."

"We promise." Sebastian and Abel said in unison.

Jorge took a breath before beginning. "Last night, after work, I got into my car and there was a text message on my phone."

He paused, closing his eyes, then continued. "It was from Dad."

Sebastian gasped, Abel's eyes widened.

Dad?

"What did it say?" Sebastian asked.

"He said he wanted to talk to me."

"Did you?" Abel questioned.

Jorge shook his head. "No. And I don't want to. I've told y'all before that things were tough when he was around but I never elaborated. Honestly, I still don't want to completely. I'm traumatized from the awful ways he's acted and the shitty things he's done. I don't want to talk about him and I want us to keep acting like he never existed."

"We won't." Sebastian answered quickly. "We trust you. If you say he's bad news, we'll keep our distance."

Abel nodded.

Go back to pretending he never existed. That'll be easy. I don't even know him.

"I love you guys. It's my job to keep you safe and I believe part of that is protecting you from him. I know I never talked about him but he was a monster."

My dad the monster. Almost sounds like a book I'd check out from the library.

"In the interest of fairness, I'll ask this once." Jorge said. "Do you want to meet him?"

"No." Sebastian said.

Then Abel. "No."

"Okay." Jorge reached over for the breakfast. "Now let's never bring him up again."

"C'mon Abel, let's go get our food and come eat in here with Jorge." Sebastian said, hopping off the bed.

Abel trailed him as they walked back to the kitchen.

I can't believe it. Nine years and out of nowhere he contacts Jorge. I don't even remember him. I mean how could I, right? I was only one when he left.

Truthfully Abel often thought about his father. They were never very positive thoughts, however.

No use worrying about someone who abandoned us. Can't miss what was never there.

Thinking about his father made him angry. Everybody else got to have their fathers or at least that's how it felt. But Abel had to go through life without his.

I don't need him. Piece of...

He looked around, almost as if he was worried someone would hear his thoughts.

...shit.

He giggled to himself, grabbed his food and orange juice, and headed back to Jorge's room.

Within moments his father was gone from his mind again. No use thinking of what can't be.

Sebastian VI

Sebastian felt the blood rush to his head as he hung upside down from the monkey bars.

Though he tried to avoid it, his thoughts kept drifting back to his father.

I can't believe Dad contacted Jorge.

It's all he had been thinking about ever since his older brother had shared the news with him the day before.

He didn't want to meet his father. He had no interest in reconnecting with the man that had not only abandoned him, but also his brothers and mother.

Yet, his father continued to reappear in his thoughts.

It left him conflicted. He hated his father but the whole situation was so crazy. Gone for nine years and then back out of nowhere?

He wanted to know why.

If there's one thing Sebastian hated, it was unanswered questions.

Maybe it's okay to not know everything. Especially when it's related to him.

But still the nagging feeling continued to poke at him.

Why did he care so much about the actions of someone he didn't even remember?

He was running cycles in his head, trying to work it out of his mind.

Maybe he just wants to come back and ruin our lives. We're doing good without him. Good enough, at least.

Maybe he found out how everything's going great without him and that really pissed him off. He wants to come back and upset everything.

Maybe he...

Maybe.

It was the word that kept popping up over and over again. It almost felt inescapable.

He let out a deep sigh.

No matter how much I think it over, I won't know why. I may never know.

I have to be okay with that.

He released his grip on the monkey bars and tumbled to the ground.

Picking himself up and dusting his clothes, he began to leave the park.

I wonder how Jorge and Abel are handling this. I'd ask but since we agreed to move on I figure that'll do more harm than good.

Do they think like me? Repeating the same questions over and over? Wanting to know why?

Or do they just accept the uncertainty and move on?

Oh great. More questions.

He slapped his forehead lightly and picked up his pace to a quick jog.

If I can't ask my brothers, maybe I can get Raul's opinion on all this.

He smiled, thinking of his boyfriend before remembering that he and his family left town for the weekend.

Aw man and he said they wouldn't have service out there either. Guess I really am alone with my thoughts, at least for now.

Admittedly he didn't mind too much. He liked having time to himself though, without his beloved office building, he'd been using the park to collect his thoughts.

He liked arguing with himself, thinking of all the possibilities for any given situation. Imagining scenarios that would never happen.

Though the questions involving his father were much less fun.

It's weird to feel so...disconnected from my parents. To not have them in my life.

My mom's dead and my dad's a deadbeat. All I can rely on are my brothers and I love them but at the same time that sting of being parentless never really goes away.

He thought back to his argument with Jorge after they ate at Olive Garden.

I was such a jerk. Telling him he's not my parent. Ignoring his appeals to talk things through. I don't even know why I got so defensive.

I guess it was mostly cause of all the Raul stuff. Still, I feel bad for the way I acted.

It may be true that Jorge isn't my parent but I shouldn't be so disrespectful. He's gone above and beyond as a brother.

With mom gone he's really stepped up. He takes care of me, Abel too. I need to be more careful with my attitude.

For all the shit he gave his older brother for being temperamental, Sebastian had to admit he had his moments as well.

I don't have Gone Days like he does but I do get pretty moody sometimes. The only one that doesn't is Abel.

A smirk crossed his face as he thought of his little brother.

That kid is something else. He's so sweet compared to me and Jorge. I don't know where he gets it from.

I look at him and I feel happiness within me. Happy that I know he'll grow up to be someone special.

And his reaction to the whole gay thing as well. I have to give him credit for that. For him to be so young and so cool with it, that was the best.

He's also kept to his word. He hasn't treated me differently at all since finding out. I'm still just his annoying older brother. Still just Sebastian.

He kicked some rocks in front of him as he approached his house. Before fully reaching it, he stopped.

I'm really the luckiest guy alive to have the brothers that I do. I don't always show my appreciation the way I should or as often as I should, but I'm really and truly grateful.

***

Back in his room, Sebastian lay on his bed, staring up at the ceiling.

It had been a day with many reflections and it had felt good to be introspective.

Jorge. Abel. Raul.

Mom. Paz.

All the great people either currently or formerly in my life and I was worried about my dad?

Worried about his reasoning? About if he'd track us down?

It's useless to worry about what may or may not happen. I should be happy and live in the here and now. I need to get these what if's and shove them outta my brain.

Like Jorge said, we need to move on like we were already doing.

With a determined smile, Sebastian decided to see the bright side of things, whenever possible.

He was set on moving forward, just like his brothers.

Unfortunately, it didn't last long.

Over and over it kept reappearing in his head.

No! No more! It's time to move on!

I'm moving on!

So then, why did he still keep thinking of his father?

Abel VI

"Here, pass me the glue and I'll be able to add the stars." Sidney said.

Abel rummaged through the small container of craft items each pair had been given.

"Here ya go." He said, passing her the bottle.

It was Project Day in class and, thankfully, they were allowed to choose their partners.

As soon as Mr. Ramirez gave the go ahead, Abel and Sidney had made eye contact, pairing up without even having to say a word.

"What else do you think it's missing?" She asked, holding up their poster on constellations.

"Hmm." Abel said, grabbing hold of the poster and looking it over. "Looks good to me. I don't really think anything else needs to be added."

"You sure?"

"I think so."

Sidney took the poster back, flipped it over and signed her name. "Alright we'll sign it and I'll look it over one more time."

She slid it over to Abel who quickly scribbled out his name.

I wish I had better handwriting. Last year Ms. Johnson said it looked like chicken scratch. Whatever that means.

The memory made him a bit sad, she had said it in front of the whole class, causing him much embarrassment.

"Hey Abel?"

He looked to Sidney. "What's up?"

"I had something I kinda wanted to talk to you about." She said, a bit apprehensive.

Her tone made Abel nervous.

"What is it?" He asked.

"Do you know a boy named Thomas Marquez?"

"Oh." Abel muttered. "Yeah I know him. Or at least I used to, why?"

"Well, I was sitting near him in gym while you ran over to get us our jump ropes and I heard him saying some mean things about you."

"What did he say?"

"He was making fun of the way you run."

"What's wrong with how I run?" He asked, defensively.

"I don't think there's anything wrong with it." She answered. "But he was saying you run like a girl. Why does he not like you?"

"I don't really know." Abel said, honestly. "We used to be good friends. I thought we were. We were both friends with this awesome guy named Charlie but he moved away. Now Thomas avoids me."

"I'm sorry to hear that." Sidney said, resting her hand on his shoulder. "People can be so mean."

"I had been thinking about trying to talk to him again. Now after what you've told me, I'm not so sure I should."

"Sorry if I've messed anything up."

"Nah you haven't. He's a jerk anyways."

He handed the poster back to her and she got to work on checking their information.

When did Thomas become so mean? He used to be kinda annoying, but saying I run like a girl? What's that about?

He pensively tapped his fingers against the desk. Then he looked over at Sidney.

Well, who cares anyways. I don't need him. I've made a new friend.

"Okay!" Sidney exclaimed. "Everything looks great, I'm gonna go turn it in."

She got up and headed towards Mr. Ramirez as Abel continued to think.

I don't even feel like I have space to worry about Thomas. I have a new friend, plus all

*that other stuff going on at home. It's pointless
to be stuck on someone that's changed for the
worse.*

Truthfully his mind had been mostly filled with
thoughts of his brothers. He was worried about
them. They had seemed so shaken up about
their father's attempted contact.

Strangely, Abel himself hadn't felt worried at
all. In fact, his father had stopped appearing in
his thoughts completely. He only showed up in
passing, like the wind. Only when he thought of
Sebastian and Jorge.

*Things feel so tense now. The whole house feels
like it has this dark cloud over it. Weirdly, I
don't think Sebastian and Jorge feel it. They're
trying to move on like everything is normal,
but I can tell there's something bothering
them.*

*I'm starting to feel like the only normal person
there.*

He shook his head, finding the thought
incredulous. His brothers were tough, they'd
make it through their dark periods. It made
sense to him that they were more concerned
than him.

Abel felt like he had nothing to miss.

***

When the school day ended, Abel rushed to
beat the crowd and make it outside.

Teachers never seemed to get onto him for his brisk hallway jog and it always left him feeling a tiny bit rebellious.

It wasn't a full on run but it was faster than a normal walk.

Today however, as he sped down the hallway, he felt a foot appear in front of his leg, causing him to fall over.

He toppled to the ground, his binder and papers spreading out all across the floor.

"Ow!" He shouted, his elbow hurting as he heard laughs behind him.

"You should watch where you're going." Thomas said with a laugh, walking by the knocked boy.

"What's your problem?!" Abel said, gathering up his papers. "You could've hurt me!"

"Could've? I should've!" Thomas said, kicking one of Abel's papers aside. "Get over it."

He started to walk off, high five-ing his friends as Abel seethed with anger.

Stupid Thomas!

As the pain rushed through his arm, Abel quietly picked up his papers. His eyes felt watery.

He looked over and saw Thomas staring at him from far off. His face looked downcast, before turning away and continuing to walk.

Jerk.

Abel felt a single tear stroll down his cheek.

Don't cry, Abel. Not here. At least wait till you get home.

But he couldn't help himself. His tear quickly turned to sniffles, before his breath quickened. He softly began to sob as he finished picking up his items.

With a wipe to his nose, he sadly began to walk outside.

He didn't feel like jogging anymore.

***

The strong wind hit him as he stepped off the bus. While he was no longer crying, he still felt sad.

What a way to ruin a perfectly good day.

<u>Jorge VI</u>

Jorge's hands shook as he stared at the computer screen in front of him.

He didn't know why he had done it, but he'd tracked down his father's profile on Facebook.

Now, staring at the profile picture before him, he felt shivers run up and down his back.

Nine years. Nine years without seeing that face. And now here it is. Right in front of me.

Even in picture form he felt overwhelmed when confronted with his father's visage.

I shouldn't have looked him up. When I talked to the boys I told them we were moving on. But the curiosity got the better of me, and now, here I am.

He couldn't even force himself to look away. Especially when he noticed something else.

Though the profile was set to private, there was one bit of information available to him.

A line below his father's name. His place of employment. Stevenson & Co Roofing.

And when he clicked it he was transported to the job's page.

And an address.

His work address.

Jorge felt his head rush with emotion and fear.

I know where he's at. That's just a town over. He's 40 minutes away from us.

He gulped and clicked the address link, which sent him to a map page.

The whole situation suddenly felt realer than ever before. He felt a panic within him.

This isn't going to go away. Even if he never contacts me again, just the idea of him being so close...

He's like this monster that lives inside my head. This beast that I can't fully rid myself of.

I'm not gonna be able to carry on.

He couldn't explain why this had shaken him so bad, other than the obvious reawakening of his old traumas. Other than that, his father had taken on an almost mythical like placement in his head.

He clicked backwards, back to his father's profile.

It felt like the profile picture was burrowing into his soul.

He scrolled down but found it empty, completely privated and locked down.

He returned to the top and kept staring. It wasn't healthy, but he couldn't look away.

Putting a face back onto the man that had abandoned him was intoxicating. Possessing.

"That's him isn't it?"

The voice from behind startled him, causing him to jump in his chair.

He turned to find Sebastian standing in his doorway.

"Seb, you scared the crap out of me!"

Sebastian stepped forward. "That's Dad, right?"

Jorge sighed. "Yes it is. I don't know why I tracked him down or what I'm hoping to gain from any of this. I just had to see him."

"Can I be honest with you?" Sebastian said, resting himself on Jorge's shoulder.

"Of course."

"I haven't been able to stop thinking of him. No matter how hard I try to change my thoughts, he just won't leave them."

"I've been having the same problem." Jorge said, defeated. "And I think by doing this I've made it worse."

"Cause of the picture?"

"That and this." He said, waving the computer arrow over the address. "I've found where he works."

"Woah."

"The worst part is he's only 40 minutes away. He's literally so close to us."

"Has he tried to contact you again?"

"No. Not since that time after work. Knowing he's so close has me scared that he'll come try and visit."

"Does he know where we live?"

"I don't think so. Still if it was so easy for me to find this about him, who knows what he knows about us. I still don't even know how he got my phone number."

"What are you going to do with it?"

Jorge turned to look at Sebastian, confused. "With what?"

"This information, like his address and stuff."

"I wasn't planning on doing anything with it. What good does a work address do for me. It doesn't help get him out of my head."

"Maybe it can."

Jorge grew stern. "What are you getting at, Seb?"

"It's just, well, we've built him up as this big monster inside of our head. This...thing without form. Maybe seeing him in person will help lay him to rest."

"Are you fucking nuts? You want to meet up with him?" Jorge exclaimed.

"No!" Sebastian said, defensively. "You're misunderstanding me. I DON'T want to meet him. I just think maybe if we scoped out his workplace, did some spying, maybe it would help stop him from being this...monster inside our head."

"Seb you've said a lot of crazy things before, but I literally think this is your worst idea ever."

"So what's the alternative then Jorge?! We keep living how we are, with him in our heads? Sleepless and afraid of this ghost from our childhood? I don't want that! I want to put him to rest and I don't think we can do that just by sitting around and always thinking of him!" Sebastian shouted.

"And you think spying on him will fix that? Just seeing this picture of him has guaranteed me many more nights of no sleep! You're idea is stupid, Seb."

Sebastian was taken aback, hurt. "So I'm stupid then right? Stupid for wanting to try something to help me move on?"

"I didn't mean it like that."

"I think you did. What do you have to gain from hiding in this house all day? We are

NEVER gonna be able to move past this if that's all we're doing. What I'm suggesting may be stupid, may be crazy, but it's better than what we've been doing. I won't sit around and do nothing and let this consume me."

"Seb-"

"No, don't Seb me. Let me finish what I need to say. We've let him become this mythological monster in our head. He's become this inhuman thing in our brains. If we spy on him, see him doing normal shit, maybe that'll fix it. Maybe we'll stop seeing him like that and start seeing him as the normal shitty human he is. I don't want to meet him. I don't want to speak to him. I just want to humanize him and move on."

Jorge remained silent for a beat before speaking.

"First of all, I'm sorry. I should've never used the word stupid. You're not stupid, your idea isn't stupid, I'm sorry."

"It's okay." Sebastian answered.

"But I just don't think I can go through with this. Not because it's a bad idea, but because I'm afraid."

"I am too, Jorge. I'm so afraid. But you know what scares me more?"

"What?"

"The idea of living in fear for the rest of my life. Of letting him be this monstrous thing inside my head. I want to get it over with. See him for what he really is. A human. A bad human, but a human."

Jorge thought it over. "I understand."

Sebastian leaned against the computer chair. "So what are we gonna do about it."

"We'll go. Do your plan and scope him out. Just you and me though."

"Why not Abel?"

"Because he's fine. He's adjusting to this way better than you and me. I don't want this to be the thing that messes him up."

"Alright then. Just you and me."

"Tomorrow, while Abel is at school, we'll go."

He held up his hand, pinkie extended.

Sebastian did the same and the promise was formed.

Sebastian VII

Sebastian took a sip of his Powerade as Jorge pulled into the parking spot.

The brothers were across the street from the Stevenson & Co Roofing office. Tense, they sat in silence, watching the front doors for any sign of their father.

"I still don't know how I feel about this." Jorge said, curtly. "But I'm going to trust your judgment."

"Thank you." Sebastian said. "We'll see him and then bounce."

"And if he doesn't come into work today?"

"Then it's a sign we should just let things be."

"You believe in signs?" Jorge asked, curious.

"I do. What's meant to be is meant to be. Sometimes we get warnings and sometimes we don't. Do you?"

Jorge thought for a moment. "I don't know. I've always considered myself to be pragmatic and realistic. I'd like to believe in stuff like fate and signs, but I don't know that I can."

"That doesn't surprise me."

"Why's that?"

"You've always been thoughtful with stuff. I figured you wouldn't allow yourself to believe in things like that."

"Is that a bad thing?"

"I don't think it is." Sebastian said with a head shake. "I think it's good that we have different views. It keeps us balanced."

"I don't know if I'd describe us as balanced." Jorge said with a laugh.

"Maybe not, but it would be pretty sad if we were all cynical and non believers. Aside from that I think I'm overall pretty in the middle on stuff."

"So I'm on one end and I'm guessing Abel is on the other?"

"And I'm in the middle."

"Seb?"

"Yeah?"

"Where'd this idea come from? This whole thing about seeing dad physically to demythologize him? It's a pretty heady idea for a 13 year old."

"To be honest it just kinda popped into my mind. I think we've let him become this big bad monster in our head. Something otherworldly. We need to come back down to Earth."

Jorge nodded. "I'd be lying if I said I wasn't afraid he'd see us."

"He won't. We're far away and it's not like he's expecting us here. Plus we got these." Sebastian said, holding up two pairs of binoculars.

"You really think of everything, don't you?"

"I'm good at planning." Sebastian said with a smile.

"Yet you're always late for everything."

"Apples to oranges, hermano. Just cause I'm good at planning doesn't mean I have good time management skills. My executions can be a little faulty sometimes."

"If you were really good at planning you'd plan on how to be early."

Sebastian shrugged. "I don't see it that way."

"And if this doesn't work? You said we'd work on moving on but how exactly do you plan on doing that?"

"It's too early to worry about that. We'll get through this first and then see where we're at."

"Can I have a sip of your Powerade?"

"Sure." Sebastian said, tossing it to him. "No little fishies."

"I haven't even eaten anything. You're expecting backwash from a clean mouth?"

"Don't trust you."

Jorge laughed as he took a sip. "You and Abel were the ones who used to leave a bunch of backwash in my drinks. It was so gross."

"That was mostly Abel, I take no responsibility for that."

"Uh huh." Jorge said, handing the bottle back to Sebastian. "You were just as bad as he was."

"No way."

"Dude you definitely were. You were a monster at Abel's age. I remember cause it was only 3 years ago."

"Sure I was more mischievous but Abel can be a slob sometimes. I'm much more clean."

"When's the last time you've even tidied up your room?"

"When's the last time you did?"

"Fair enough." Jorge said.

"I used to sometimes feel a little left out cause you and Abel were so similar. Goody two shoes and all that."

"Left out?"

"Well yeah. I felt like maybe you two were closer since you had more in common."

"Seb, are you serious?"

"What?"

"I'm way closer to you. I love you both equally with all my heart, but there's no denying that you're the one I feel most connected to. Hell, sometimes *I* feel left out."

"Why do you?"

"Cause I think you and Abel are closer." Jorge admitted.

"I love you both equally though. I do spend more time with Abel but that's just cause you work. All 3 of us would spend all day together if I had it my way."

Jorge sighed. "Yeah I wish we could too. But I have to support you guys and that's hard to do with no money. I almost lost my job the other day when I didn't go in."

"How'd you manage to keep it?"

"Just made up a friend's funeral."

Sebastian laughed. "Jeez that's kinda dark bro."

"Hey but it worked!" Jorge exclaimed.

The brothers shared a laugh before Sebastian grew serious.

"Hey Jorge there's been something on my mind lately. Something I wanted to talk with you about. Regarding me."

"What is it?" Jorge said, concerned.

"Well it's-"

Suddenly, Sebastian stopped, mid sentence.

"Look!" He shouted.

Across the street, walking to the front door of the building, was a man.

"Quick! The binoculars!" Jorge said.

Sebastian put them up to his eyes and saw him.

Their father.

It felt like everything went in slow motion. It was surreal to be there staring at their father in action. He was about to enter the building when he stopped to take a phone call.

Watching him pace back and forth with whoever was on the other end. Leaning against the building, kicking a pebble, squishing an ant.

So...human.

Not a monster. Not a beast. Not a ghost.

A human.

The way he leaned, running his palm over the top of his head. Lowering his hand and hooking his thumb into his belt loop. Balancing one foot by the heel.

He hung up the phone, wiped his nose with the back of his sleeve and walked into the building.

Sebastian lowered the binoculars and looked at Jorge.

His older brother's eyes were red with tears. As they looked at each other, Jorge unbuckled his seat belt and reached over to hug Sebastian.

The brothers embraced for what felt like forever before letting go of each other.

Silently, they left the parking lot.

Jorge VII

Jorge watched as Sebastian slathered his midday pancakes in syrup.

That boy loves breakfast for lunch.

Jorge looked down at his food. Some simple chicken strips thrown haphazardly onto the plate, fries bunched to the side with a small dollop of ketchup.

Taking one of his fries, dipping it and then biting, Jorge felt a strange sense of calm over himself.

I can't believe we saw him. I can't believe we did it.

"You doing ok?" Sebastian asked, stuffing a forkful into his mouth.

Jorge nodded. "I'm glad I listened to you, Seb. I think I'm feeling better already."

"Told you." Sebastian said with a smile. "But thanks for trusting my plan."

"Guess it all worked out in the end."

"Guess so."

They sat in silence for a moment, picking at their food and eating.

It wasn't tension that kept them silent, rather, it was peace. For the first time in quite awhile they felt like their worries had subsided.

Even if it was only for a moment.

"Abel will kill us if he finds out we came here without him." Sebastian said, continuing to eat.

"Yeah, this definitely has to stay between you and me."

"Do you think that's messed up of us?"

Jorge thought it over a minute. "Nah. Nothing wrong with taking a day to ourselves. I'll do something for just me and him soon. That'll even it up."

"Maybe I'll take him to a movie, if that's alright with you."

"Of course. When have I ever stopped y'all from going to the movies?" Jorge said with a chuckle.

"Yeah but I know you love going."

"That's true but it'll be good for you to do something with him. Just the two of you. I'll take him out to eat, you take him to the movies."

"Sounds like a plan."

Admittedly I do feel bad for Abel. We'll make it up to him, though. I don't mean to leave him out but this is something that needed to be done between Seb and I.

Abel's strong. Stronger than I could've imagined. He hasn't been bothered by our father's reappearance. I didn't want to risk bringing him here and triggering him.

"Hey Seb?"

"Yeah?"

"Back in the car, before we saw dad, you were gonna tell me something. What was it?"

Sebastian paused for a moment.

He looks...concerned?

"Seb? Is everything okay?"

"Yeah." Sebastian finally answered. "Everything's fine. What I was gonna tell you, it's not important. Well I mean it is, but it's not something that needs to be said right away. Especially in a crowded diner. I promise when the time is right, I'll tell you."

"But you're okay?"

"Yup. Don't worry Jorge. It's nothing serious."

Not the most comforting words, but I'll have to take his word for it. What's that boy hiding though?

"Can I ask you something?" Sebastian said.

"Sure, go ahead."

"I was thinking about a little over a year ago, before mom passed. You were dating that girl Beatrice. What ever happened to her?"

Jorge smiled when he heard her name.

Beatrice.

"We broke up. I didn't really tell you guys, although I'm sure you picked up on it."

"She used to come by all the time. When she stopped coming, we assumed you guys were through but we were afraid to ask."

"Yeah." Jorge said, sadly. "She used to love coming around. Mom loved her and she was so good with you and Abel."

"So what happened?" Sebastian asked.

"Well, Mom died and my life kinda took a turn of sorts. I had to work more, take care of y'all. I didn't have time for a relationship."

"Was she mad?"

"No, she understood. She offered to stick around, try and make things work. I just felt like I couldn't. I didn't have it within me. I felt like such a black hole of sadness, I couldn't pull her in."

"Wow." Sebastian said, laying his fork down. "That's sad. What happened to her then?"

"I still see her from time to time on Facebook. She's doing good, working mostly. I haven't talked to her since after mom's funeral, though."

"Will you?"

"Will I what?" Jorge asked, confused.

"Will you talk to her again?"

"Oh." Jorge said. "Nah probably not. It's been a year, she's moving on. Plus I don't think it's a good time for me to start up an old relationship."

"Why not?"

"I'm still so busy, I hardly have any time."

"Jorge," Sebastian said, "you're always gonna be busy. That's just who you are. From what you said, she was willing to be flexible and try to work on the relationship even with everything going on in your life. Maybe it's worth trying for again."

"I don't know. I do miss her, but I just don't think it's realistic."

"Why?"

"Because it's been a year. She wasn't mad when I broke things off but I could tell it hurt her. Why should I bring up old feelings again?"

"Look, she really really liked you Jorge. I could tell, Abel could tell...Mom could tell. Everybody could. You guys were so good together. I think it's worth a shot."

Sebastian reached over and took hold of Jorge's hand.

"I'm saying this, brother to brother." Sebastian said. "Give it another shot. Come back to life."

Jorge felt himself swelling with emotion.

Maybe he's right.

"You know what, Seb? Okay. When we're back home I'm gonna work up the courage to hit her up again. I'm gonna try."

Sebastian smiled. "That's all I'm asking for, brother. You can do it."

The brothers continued to eat, not speaking, but not needing to.

Things felt safe again. There was a closeness there that had been strengthened by this trip.

Jorge was grateful that he let Sebastian talk him into coming.

Seeing their father, bonding.

Talking about Beatrice.

Jorge's heart fluttered at the thought of her.

You can't just fade away.

His mother's words reappeared.

He had spent a year fading.

Time to reform.

Abel VII

Abel excitedly tapped his fingers against the cafeteria table.

It had become a highlight of his day to spend lunchtime with Sidney. Sure they saw each other in class first, but sometimes there wasn't much room to talk.

Recently, Mr. Ramirez had changed the seating chart, leaving Abel and Sidney separated on opposite ends of the room.

Bad luck getting stuck next to Alberto.

Alberto was one of Thomas' friends and he made sure to annoy Abel whenever possible.

But now I can just relax with Sidney, hang out, eat. Back to basics.

As he continued to wait for her, he opened up his sketchbook and began to doodle.

Nothing exemplary or too interesting. Often times he enjoyed just putting pencil to paper and seeing where a line took him.

This time it seemed to be something monstrous. He liked drawing monsters the most of all.

"Hey Abel."

He looked up to see Sidney standing over him, backpack held against her chest.

"Oh hey Sid! Took you awhile today!" Abel said, scooting over to make room.

Sidney smiled. "Actually I kinda needed to talk to you."

"Oh?"

"Yeah, well y'know how Mr. Ramirez gave us new seats?" She said.

"Yeah," Abel answered, "what about them?"

"I've been sitting by Jocelyn and we've been getting along so awesomely and she's invited me to sit with her and her friends in the outer area at lunch."

"Oh so we're moving out there?" Abel asked, a little thrown off.

"Umm...well, I am. I'm really sorry but they don't like boys sitting with them, it gets kind of awkward. They like to gossip and stuff like that it'd probably be pretty boring for you."

"Maybe not, I mean we could try it out."

Sidney sighed. "I'm sorry Abel. I just think I'd be better out there. You're so cool and sweet, but I think it's better for me to try having some friends. You understand right?"

Abel felt tears form in the corners of his eyes.

No I don't understand. I thought we were friends!

That's what he wanted to say.

"Yeah I get it." Was what he really ended up saying.

"Thanks! I'm sure we'll see each other around and stuff. And thank you for keeping me company, you'll find your own group soon!" She said, turning away.

Abel held up a hand, giving up a kind of defeated wave, but Sidney didn't even notice. She was gone in the blink of an eye, out the door.

Wow.

Abel moved his sketchbook and lunchbox to the side, crossed his arms on the table and lowered his head.

She just left, like it was nothing.

Like our friendship was nothing.

He sobbed quietly into his arms, unable to comprehend why she'd leave him like that.

All cause they don't allow boys to sit with them? Or is it because of me?

The thought made him even sadder.

It has to be me. I didn't have friends before her, I made one, then I lost her. All cause of me.

He felt a rush of emotion throughout his body, his stomach twisted up. He hadn't even eaten anything.

I can't keep a friend to save my life. Except for Charlie.

He thought back to his best friend and grew angry.

Why did you have to move?! Why couldn't you just stay here with me?!

He felt selfish for his inner outburst. The world didn't revolve around him. Charlie and his family had moved to care for his ailing grandma who lived 2 states away.

They had to move. I get that, but it doesn't make it hurt any less.

He lifted his head up a bit and began to flip through his sketchbook.

He landed on a page with 2 figures drawn. It was Abel and Sidney and above it he had written:

BEST FRIENDS

in big bubble letters. He had planned to give her the drawing once he had finished it up.

Guess I can't now.

With anger pumping through his hands he ripped the page from his sketchbook and began to tear it to pieces.

He had never ripped his art before. Even when he drew something that didn't come out quite right he'd pack it away somewhere.

Today, however, he felt angry.

He wanted to destroy something.

Before he knew it, the page was torn into tiny confetti sized parts. He wanted his former picture to be unrecognizable.

I don't need Sidney. I was fine being alone, I'm used to it.

No need for friends, I can make it through school all by myself. Everybody just ends up hurting me.

He flipped to more pages, ripping them out one by one and crumpling them up.

Stupid art. Stupid friends. Stupid Abel.

He continued to tear the pages before getting up, grabbing the whole sketchbook and tossing it into the trash.

I don't need it!

He sat back down at the table and opened his lunchbox. He took furious bites of his sandwich, feeling like an animal.

Stupid, fat Abel.

He didn't know why he was insulting himself. He just felt mad at everything and everybody.

He wanted to blame Sidney, he wanted to blame himself, he wanted to blame Charlie, and Thomas, and Alberto, and Mr. Ramirez.

Everybody.

And worst of all? This anger just made him feel worse.

He never liked being angry. He didn't have the temperament of his brothers, he was usually much calmer and well put together.

I'm not usually like this, so why can't I get over it?

Maybe it was the feeling of betrayal. The feeling of having one good thing to look forward to and then losing it.

The feeling of lost hope.

Hope of having a friend. Not even friends, just one. At least one.

But no, with today's transgression, Abel felt like he'd be lonely forever.

It's pointless to get my hopes up.

I have to understand that people don't want to be around me. Other than my brothers, who are forced to.

Nobody wants to spend time with the fat loser.

Abel finished his food and put his head back down.

Sebastian VIII

Sebastian ran excitedly down the sidewalk, up to the entrance of the coffee shop.

Inside, at a table back towards the corner, sat Raul, scrolling through his phone.

"Hey!" Sebastian said, pulling the chair out to sit. "Sorry I took awhile, I had to finish up my chores."

Raul clicked his phone closed and laid it down. "No problem. I actually just got here a couple of minutes ago, I was worried I'd be too early and I ended up being too late."

"Still earlier than me." Sebastian said, smiling as he waved down the server. "You could've gotten away with it."

"How can I help you?" The server asked.

"I'll just have a hot chocolate." Sebastian said. "And you?"

Raul shook his head. "I'm good. My stomach hasn't been the best lately."

The server nodded and walked off.

"So what's been going on in your life?" Raul asked, leaning forward on his elbows. "I feel like we haven't had much time to ourselves."

"Yeah I know! Things just got so busy out of nowhere. I've been wanting to talk to you. Me and Jorge went to go see our Dad. Well, from afar, not like meet him or anything."

Raul widened his eyes. "Jeez, really? How'd that go?"

"It was...good. I mean, I feel better. Still it was admittedly kinda intense."

"I bet. How'd Jorge handle it?"

"About the same as me. I really felt like I bonded with him." Sebastian paused for a beat. "Actually I even almost came out to him."

"No way! What stopped you?"

"Seeing our Dad took us out of the moment and by the time it passed I lost my courage."

Raul smiled and outstretched his hand, resting it over Sebastian's. "You're courageous for even attempting it. That's a big step for you! You'll get back to it someday."

"It's really starting to feel like it'll be sooner rather than later. I think I'm almost ready."

"Has Abel said anything about it?"

"Not really. Things have been good with him in that department."

"And in other departments?" Raul asked, curiously.

"He's seemed so sad lately. Me and Jorge have tried to get him to say what's wrong, but he just keeps telling us he doesn't want to talk about it."

"What do you think is upsetting him?"

"I don't really know." Sebastian said, taking his hot chocolate from the server. "Thank you."

"No problem." She said as she walked off.

As Sebastian lifted his hot chocolate to take a sip, Raul adjusted his hair and leaned back in his chair a bit.

"Poor Abel. I hope he's able to open up to y'all soon."

"I hope so too." Sebastian said. "I miss how cheerful he used to be."

"You think his weight is the issue?" Raul asked.

Sebastian set his cup down. "What're you talking about?"

"Well, y'know..."

Sebastian grew confused. "I don't think I do. What are you trying to say?"

An awkward laugh escaped Raul. "I don't mean nothing mean, it's just he's pretty...chunky and I know that when people are overweight they can have low self esteem. Maybe that's what's got him down? Or maybe he's being bullied over it?"

"I don't think it's that." Sebastian said, pushing his hot chocolate to the side.

Not so thirsty anymore.

"Raul, I'm gonna be honest. I'm not really comfortable with you referring to my brother's weight."

"What? I wasn't trying to be an asshole. He's overweight, that's just a fact. It doesn't mean I'm making fun of him, I just think it could be why he's been so down."

"It doesn't matter if that's why, I'm asking *you* not to bring it up again."

"Why is this such a big deal to you?" Raul asked. "I didn't say anything bad about him."

"I didn't like your tone when you said it. You made it sound like there was something wrong with him."

"I mean there kind of is, isn't there? He's pretty big for a ten year old. I love the kid but he's big. That's just how he is and it's whatever. It might be causing problems for him."

Sebastian was stunned. "I've never heard you talk like this. It's really, really off putting."

"Me? Off putting? Just for saying Abel is over weight?"

"Stop. Saying. That. My brother is amazing the way he is. Whatever problems he's having, even weight related, that's problems the world has

145

with him. He doesn't deserve whatever is happening to him."

"And I agree! I'm sure it's some real pieces of shit bullying him! But I don't think I've said nothing wrong or untrue here."

"You're completely missing my point." Sebastian said. "You don't get to comment on my brother's weight. Ever."

"Sebastian, please." Raul reached out to take hold of Sebastian's hand. "He's like my little brother too. You know I care about him. I was just trying to say that his weight problems might be the cause of his issues."

Sebastian snatched his hand away. "I gotta go."

"I'm sorry if something I've said upset you." Raul said, standing. "Let me walk you home."

Sebastian turned away and was out the door before Raul could reach him.

***

The audacity! Nobody gets to mention my brother's weight. Me and Jorge don't even do it! And he didn't even really apologize.

"I'm sorry if something I've said upset you."

Not an apology for his words. Just "Sorry I said something you couldn't handle."

Talking like he knew anything about us. About Abel.

Sebastian threw open the front door and walked straight to Abel's room.

Abel sat up, surprised.

"Sebastian? How'd your date go?"

Sebastian ran over and grabbed his brother, pulling him into a tight hug.

"Listen to me. If anybody, ANYBODY, makes you feel like shit, don't let them! You are so freaking amazing, the most amazing kid I've ever known! You deserve to be treated good and I hope you never forget that." He tightened the hug. "I love you little brother. Just the way you are. You're better than me, better than Jorge. You're the best of us. I'm beyond proud of you. Mom would've been too."

He felt Abel crying into his shoulder.

Sebastian sat there all night, cradling his brother.

Jorge VIII

"Hello?"

"Uh, hey, Bea. It's...it's me."

"Jorge? Oh wow. I wasn't expecting this. At all. Is everything okay?"

"Yeah everything's fine. I wanted to call you up and ask if maybe you'd be down to meet up sometime? I have a lot I wanted to discuss."

There had been a slight pause.

"Of course we can meet up. I've missed you, Jorge."

"I've missed you too, Bea."

Jorge kept replaying the conversation in his head as he sat down at the restaurant.

From where he was, he had a direct view to the entrance.

Any minute now she'd walk in, just the thought of it left Jorge breathless.

Calm down. Catch yourself, don't overreact. It's Bea, you used to be so comfortable around her. Things can go back to that.

Still Jorge felt apprehensive. He tapped his fingers against the table and looked towards the entrance.

Just as he was about to pull out his phone to distract himself, he saw her.

Bea.

Just as beautiful as ever.

They locked eyes as she approached the table. She flashed a smile, Jorge felt butterflies at the sight of it.

He stood from the table and met her for a hug. It felt good to have her in his arms again. They held each other for a moment before pulling apart.

"It's so good to see you." She said, breaking the silence.

"I'm glad you came." He said back.

They took their seats.

"It's been awhile." She said. "But understandably so, of course."

"I'm sorry I never called. Times have been pretty tough."

"I'm sure. Have you been holding up okay?"

He paused, thinking it over. "I guess. Things were pretty bad for awhile, but slowly they're getting better."

"That makes me so happy to hear. I was really worried about you, but I understood that you needed space. I hope it doesn't upset you for me to say this, but I really missed you. And your family too. You're mom was an amazing woman."

A small smile crept onto Jorge's face. "She loved you. When she passed I felt like I couldn't handle being around anyone. I didn't want to pull you down with me."

"You wouldn't have." She said. "I loved you so much Jorge. I still do. You're in my thoughts often. I'm glad you took your time, and I'm also glad you finally reached out."

"I'm glad I reached out too. Being here with you, everything feels brighter. I wish I hadn't stayed away so long."

Bea smiled. "It's okay. You needed to heal. How have Seb and Abel been?"

"They've been good, better than me actually. We all struggled for awhile but I think we've come out of this with stronger bonds than ever. Seb was actually the one that set me straight about calling you."

"Aw, he was a great kid. He must be taller than the last time I saw him."

"It has been a year, they've had to do quite a bit of growing up in that time."

"And Abel?"

"Well remember how you used to love how positive he was? He's still that kid. He seemed to be going through a rough patch a couple days ago but I think Seb helped him through it.

I found them holding each other, sleeping, when I got home from work."

"That's so cute! I love that you all are still so close. I used to love watching you guys interact. It was like the family I always wanted."

"The boys will be excited to see you again."

"And I'll be excited to see them." She said. "Y'know how my home life was. Alcoholic parents, being an only child. It was hard for me. When I started dating you, I felt like I joined the family I've always wanted. It was hard to have to separate myself."

Jorge felt taken aback. "Bea, I'm so sorry. I never even thought of that. I feel so stupid."

"Don't beat yourself up over it. Like I said, I understood. I knew one day we'd reconnect." She said, reaching across the table to hold Jorge's hand.

"I was worried about picking things up again. I didn't know if you had moved on."

"I did. I have a new career, new apartment, new cat. But I never moved on from loving you. No matter how many changes my life went through, I still wanted you in it."

"You didn't have to wait for me."

"I wanted to." She said.

***

Outside the restaurant, after dinner, Jorge and Bea stood outside.

They were there, hand in hand, taking in the moment. Bea turned to look at him.

"So we're doing this then?" She asked. "Picking up where we left off?"

"I want to." Jorge said. "Do you?"

Bea smiled and pulled Jorge in for a kiss. "Of course I do."

As they pulled away, he looked at her beautiful brown eyes. He had missed them.

"Are you heading home now?" He asked. "Or should we continue this date elsewhere?"

She smirked and pulled him in for another kiss. "I know where I wanna go."

***

As the day turned into night Jorge looked over at the passenger side of his car where Bea sat, staring out the window.

I was an idiot for ending things. I closed myself off from everybody, from the whole world. This is what I needed.

She's what I needed.

She turned to look at him excitedly as they approached the house.

Pulling into the driveway, Jorge noticed a hint of tears in Bea's eyes.

"It's just like I remember. I almost feel like I'm gonna walk in and she'll greet me."

"I still feel like that too." Jorge said.

With a sigh of sadness, Bea opened her door. She took a deep breath, climbed out and began to walk towards the front door.

Jorge followed her, grabbed her hand, squeezed it and reached to turn the knob.

The door opened as Sebastian and Abel sat at the kitchen table.

"Hey guys!" Jorge said. "Look who's here."

The boys looked up.

"BEA!" They exclaimed, running to hug her.

Jorge looked to her as a tear ran down her cheek.

She was back home.

Abel VIII

Abel walked into school with more confidence than he had ever had before.

Sebastian's words bounced around in his head, filling him with the courage to live his life and not care what anyone else thought.

Even though it still stung a bit to see Sidney with her new friends at lunchtime, he simply took a deep breath and moved on.

Good for her.

He liked being back to his positive self. He didn't ever want to let his anger take hold of him again. He finished up lunch and reached into his binder where an all new sketchbook was waiting for him.

He opened up to the first page and flattened it out, then found his sharpest pencil and began to doodle.

It's nice to draw again. I do regret tearing up my old one, but there's nothing to be done now. Time to start over, refreshed.

Before lunch drew to a close and recess began, he decided to head over to the library where he could be alone with his thoughts. The cafeteria was much too noisy at this time.

As he made his way down the mostly empty hallways, he noticed a figure huddled on the floor, quietly weeping.

He began to approach before realizing who it was.

"Thomas?" Abel said, approaching the hunched figure.

Thomas' head shot up quickly.

"What do you want?" He asked angrily.

"Nothing, I just...y'know noticed you sitting here, crying. I wanted to see if everything was okay."

"I'm fine." Thomas said, haughtily.

Should I go? Or should I try again?

Abel thought his options over before making his decision.

He sat down next to Thomas, laying his binder beside him.

"You can talk to me." Abel said. "We used to be friends, remember? I don't hold grudges or anything."

Thomas sighed before turning to look at Abel. "It's Alberto. He was being a jerk to me, making fun of me in front of everybody. It just felt so embarrassing to be sitting there while everybody laughed at me and cracked jokes."

How do you think I feel?

"That's too bad. I have to sit next to Alberto in class and I know he can be pretty vicious. He says stuff about me all the time."

"And I don't even know why he's like that!" Thomas exclaimed. "Sometimes everything's chill and cool and the next he's bullying me."

"I know how that feels."

There was a silent moment of tension between the boys. Abel could tell that he had laid the problem out front and that Thomas had picked up on it.

Ultimately, it was Thomas that broke the silence.

"I'm sorry." Thomas said. "I don't know why I was so mean to you. I know we used to be good friends, but when Charlie left I thought I could start over. I was gonna be different this new school year. Still, I shouldn't have acted the way I did."

"It's okay." Abel said. "Well, I mean, it's not. You were being a jerk to me. But I forgive you."

Thomas smiled. "Thanks. I think I need to stop hanging around Alberto. He's just so negative."

"Do whatever you feel is right." Abel said, standing up and gathering his stuff. "But I'm about to head to the library to draw. You're free to join me."

Thomas stood as well.

"Sounds good." He said.

***

"Hey Abel can I talk to you?" Sebastian said, poking his head into his little brother's room.

"Oh yeah of course." Abel answered, closing his sketchbook and setting it to the side.

"I've been going through some stuff lately. I didn't want to flood you with my problems but I figure it'd be good to talk."

"I'm all ears." Abel said, flicking his ears.

Sebastian laughed and sat down on the bed.

"First of all, I think I'm done with Raul. I mean, maybe. Most of the time I loved being around him and he's helped me so much, but he said some things I can't really get over. Every time I think about forgiving him I just hear his words in my head again and I'm really put off."

"Whoa, what'd he say?" Abel asked.

"I'd rather not repeat it. It was just some mean comments about someone important to me. I don't think he meant to do harm, maybe he just misspoke but it felt so...prejudiced, I guess. I'd rather move on."

Abel smacked his lips. "Why'd you even bring up him saying something if you're not gonna tell me what he said?"

"Because it's not important what he said, it's important how he made me feel!" Sebastian said with a laugh as he grabbed Abel into a playful chokehold.

"Okay! Okay! I get it!" Abel said, tapping his brother's arm.

Sebastian released him and continued.

"So for now I'll stay single. Maybe someday I'll give him another chance but I'm only 13 anyways. Plenty of guys in the future, I'm sure."

"Don't worry, if it's meant to be it's meant to be."

"And here's the other thing." Sebastian said. "I think I'm finally ready to come out to Jorge."

Abel's eyes widened. "Really? You're sure?"

Sebastian nodded.

"When are you gonna go for it?" Abel asked.

"Tonight." Sebastian answered. "I'm gonna get it over with and lay it all out. I'm gonna be honest and speak what's in my heart. As soon as he's back from his date with Bea I'm going for it."

"I'm proud of you." Abel said. "Really I am. Trust me, everything's gonna turn out alright."

Abel reached over and hugged his older brother.

"Thank you." Sebastian said. "Although I think there's been a bit too much hugging lately."

Abel laughed. "There's never enough hugging."

They pulled away from each other as Sebastian stood up from the bed.

"Okay I'm gonna go practice what I'm gonna say. Wish me luck."

"Good luck, hermano." Abel said with a wave as Sebastian left the room.

As he reopened his sketchbook, Abel couldn't help but beam with happiness.

I'm so proud of him.

Sebastian IX

Sebastian took a deep breath.

Although he felt mentally ready to come out to Jorge, he couldn't help but let his nerves get to him a bit.

It'll be okay. It'll be okay.

He picked at the couch with his nails, pulling at a little thread. He ran his hand over the fabric and felt his fingers brush over a small tear.

Paz. She loved using this couch as a scratching post.

Smiling, he remembered sitting with the chubby little gray cat and playing with her on the couch.

"Sebastian! Don't let her scratch the couch!" His mother would say. "La va a destruir!"

"Oops, sorry mom." He'd say, picking Paz up and lowering her to the floor.

Of course she'd just jump right back on.

Truthfully it made him sad to think about Paz. He really missed her and all the trouble she'd cause.

Plus thoughts of Paz led to thoughts of his mother and that made things even tougher.

The two would be forever connected in his mind.

All these things that he loved so dearly had been gone from his life in the blink of an eye. He felt like it gave him whiplash.

He sighed, a bit depressed, before hearing a car pull up outside.

Running to the window, he slightly pulled back the curtains and saw Jorge walking up to the house.

It's time.

He paused to gather his courage before sitting back down on the couch. He wanted to talk to him on here.

The door creaked open and in walked Jorge, beaming with happiness.

"Hey Seb." He said, closing the door and locking it. "You're up a little late. Sorry it took me a while to get back."

"It's okay." Sebastian said. "How's Bea?"

"She's doing great. I invited her over for dinner this weekend, she's gonna make her spaghetti, you remember it?"

"Oh yeah." Sebastian said. "I remember it being pretty good."

"She's been taking some cooking classes so it'll probably be even better. Can't wait for us all to spend some time together."

"Yeah I really missed her. I'm glad she'll be coming around more."

Just as Jorge turned to go to his room, Sebastian stopped him.

"Hey, Jorge?"

His older brother turned around. "Yeah, what's up?"

"I was hoping I could talk to you about something before you head to bed."

Jorge approached the couch and sat down. "Is everything okay?"

"Yeah everything's fine, I've just had a lot on my mind lately. A lot that I need to talk with you about. Important things."

"Is it what you were going to bring up in the car the other day?"

Sebastian nodded.

"Okay," Jorge said, "go ahead."

Now or never.

"Jorge..." Sebastian said, pausing to collect himself. "I'm gay."

His hands shook with nerves and adrenaline. He kept looking at the floor, unable to make eye contact with his older brother.

"I was dating Raul for a bit but we broke up
and I've just been scared to tell you for awhile
now. I know you're not mean or anything but I
was still scared to because you had a lot to deal
with already and I was worried this would
stress you out more. But I don't want to hide it
anymore, I want to be open with you."

He sat in silence, waiting for his brother to
react.

Then, in one swift motion, Jorge pulled him
over and embraced him into a tight hug.

"Seb," Jorge said, "of course it's okay with me.
You know that I'll love and support you no
matter what. Don't ever be afraid to tell me
something just because it might stress me out. I
would never NEVER let my problems interfere
with your well being, even if sometimes they
get the best of me. I love you so much and I
accept you for who you are."

Sebastian held onto his older brother and cried
into his chest. It felt so good to be free, to get it
all out of his system. He felt so loved, so safe.

"Thank you." He finally said. "You're the best
older brother anybody could ask for."

He looked upwards to see Jorge smiling.

"So," Jorge said, gently pulling away from the
hug, "is there anything else you need to talk
with me about?"

Sebastian shook his head. "That's pretty much
it. Also Abel knows by the way."

"How'd he find out?"

"He walked in on me and Raul kissing."

The brothers began to laugh. It felt good for all of the tension to be broken. It felt good to feel normal.

"How did he react?" Jorge asked.

"I think maybe he was a little shell shocked at first but he's been so supportive. He really is a great little brother."

A look of content grew across Jorge's face. "I'm so proud of the both of you. I look at you two and I'm reminded of how great you make my life. I just know y'all will grow up to be amazing."

"It's all thanks to you." Sebastian said. "You're the one who's helped shape us into who we are. We wouldn't be the people we are without you."

"Don't go making me cry now." Jorge said, his voice cracking. "Being you and Abel's older brother has been the best thing to ever happen to me. I don't know what I did in a past life to deserve you two, but I'm happy I did it."

Sebastian leaned in for one more hug, this one even tighter, before letting go.

"I think I'm gonna go to bed now." Sebastian said. "I've felt so tired today but I needed to get this out."

"I'm glad you did." Jorge said. "Good night, hermano."

"Good night." Sebastian said, walking towards his room.

As he made his way down the hall he could feel so much fulfillment within himself. He was truly lucky to have the life he did.

Did he deserve it?

He wasn't sure, but he hoped he did.

Abel IX

"Hey Abel." Sebastian said from outside his door. "Can I come in?"

"Yup!" Abel said. "I'm just finishing up homework."

Sebastian opened the door and ran to flop down on Abel's bed.

"You almost done?" He asked.

Abel nodded. "Yeah I'm pretty much done. Why?"

"I was thinking we could go see a movie." Sebastian said. "How does that sound?"

Abel felt himself growing excited.

"Yes! We haven't been in forever!"

Sebastian stood up with a smile. "Well finish up your homework and start getting ready. The showing is at 7, it's just gonna be me and you by the way."

"Why not Jorge?"

"He's really beat from work, but he is gonna drop us off. Plus I think it'd be nice for me and you to spend some time together. We'll go have a nice time, catch a movie, have fun in the arcade. So get ready!"

Sebastian exited the room as Abel rushed to finish his homework.

Finally we get to go to the movies again. I feel like I've been waiting to go back for forever. I wonder what we're gonna see?

Knowing Sebastian, he knew it would probably be an action film of some sort. They only ever went to horror movies with Jorge.

I think the new Batman is playing, he'll probably want to see that.

Truthfully, Abel didn't LOVE superhero movies, but he liked the experience of being in a theater. There was just an atmosphere there that was so special for him.

He preferred goofy comedies or animated films. He liked watching cartoons and imagining how they were made. The work and dedication that went into them.

He knew that when he grew up he'd love to get the opportunity to make one someday. When he had done research online, he saw how tough the industry seemed.

It felt daunting, but he knew with determination he could accomplish his goals.

I'll make something great. An amazing animated adventure. Something epic!

He finished the last problem on his homework and jumped from his chair. Rushing to his closet, he threw open the doors and rummaged through his clothes.

Most of his stuff was pretty wrinkled but he didn't really mind. He never felt too bothered by his appearance clothing wise. There were shirts that he wore often, ones with cool designs and fun characters.

Tonight however, he was going to go with a simple red t-shirt.

Pulling it over his white muscle shirt, he then grabbed some jeans and slid them on.

Within minutes he was fully dressed and ready to go.

The clock on his dresser read 6:20 meaning there was still some time. It only took around 20 minutes to get there anyways.

While Abel liked to be there as early as possible he knew that Sebastian would end up getting them there close to showtime. With Jorge driving maybe they'd get there a little earlier but Sebastian was always the last one to be dressed.

He loved waiting until the last second to get ready.

He left his room and walked to the kitchen to grab a granola bar. Jorge sat at the kitchen table, typing away at his phone.

"Damn you got ready quick!" Jorge said, looking him over. "You could've asked me to iron your stuff."

"Nah," Abel said with a laugh, "I'm fine like this."

Jorge shook his head playfully and went back to texting.

"You sure you don't want to come with us?" Abel asked him.

"I'm good." Jorge answered. "It'll be good for you two to hang out a bit. Also I was thinking me and you could go get something to eat next week."

"Just us?" Abel said.

Jorge nodded. "Just us. It's good to have one on one time every once in awhile. Also Bea's coming over for dinner this weekend."

Abel perked up. "Is she making her spaghetti?"

"Yup." Jorge said. "She remembered how much you used to love it."

"It was the best." Abel said, walking back towards the living room. "I can't wait."

As he leaned against the couch, he could feel excitement in his heart. It sucked going through so many rough patches, but it was nice to get back to some normalcy.

For the first time in a long time, Abel felt like his struggles were gone. Things still weren't perfect, but it was nice to be feeling better.

Plus, there was now spaghetti to look forward to.

Abel saw Sebastian exit the bathroom and run to his room.

"I'm almost ready! I swear!" He said, slamming his bedroom door.

Abel rolled his eyes at his silly older brother.

Always until the last minute.

He was used to it by this point. Nothing Sebastian did was surprising anymore. He liked that.

Weirdly, even things at school felt calmer than ever. Although it had been a rough start, regaining Thomas as a friend again felt good.

They continued to eat lunch and talk together and it felt just like old times.

I just wish Charlie was still around.

Losing his best friend had left the school year feeling emptier, even with the added benefits of having Thomas back and his brief friendship with Sidney.

She seemed to be doing well for herself also, given a few apparent fights with her friends. Abel was happy to see her doing better, even if he couldn't be her friend anymore.

He wasn't the type to sit around and hold grudges.

Lately he had been thinking of asking Jorge to help him track down Charlie in order to reconnect with him.

Maybe he could find his parents on Facebook, Abel vaguely recalled their names.

Maybe they'd let him talk to Abel. He wondered if Charlie missed him too.

Suddenly, there was a knock at the door.

"Hey Abel can you get that?" Jorge shouted from the kitchen.

"Yup I got it!" Abel said, running to the door.

He opened it and took a step back.

A man stood at the door and something about him seemed strangely familiar.

"Abel?" The man said. "Dios mio, you're so big now mijo."

Abel continued to stare in silence.

"What's wrong?" The man asked. "Don't recognize your own father?"

<u>Jorge IX</u>

From the kitchen doorway, Jorge felt a rush of emotions.

He didn't know how long had passed.

Seconds? Minutes?

Time didn't exist at the moment. Tunnel vision enveloped him as he stared.

His father at the door. Abel frozen in front of him.

He felt like he wanted to vomit. As if his stomach was about to drop out of him completely. Everything was in slow motion.

Then he snapped back to life.

With a brisk step forward, he began to approach the door.

"Abel, go to Sebastian's room."

"Jorge," his little brother stammered, "I-is that really..."

"Go now!"

Abel took off towards Sebastian's room. As the door shut Jorge worked up the courage to speak.

"What are you doing here?" He said, gaining the courage to look up towards his father.

"What do you mean what am I doing here?" His father said, his voice chilling Jorge to the bone. "Am I not allowed to visit my sons?"

Jorge shook his head. "No you're not. Not after 9 years."

His father sighed. "I didn't come here to fight, mijo. I came to talk. That's all."

"We don't need to talk. There's nothing to say."

"I think you're wrong about that. I think there's a lot for us to say. Aside from that, I'm not leaving till I get the chance to say it."

"Well I don't want to hear what you have to say, so leave."

"That's no way to talk to your father."

"I don't have a father!" Jorge yelled, he began to shut the door but his father blocked it with his foot.

"When were you gonna tell me that your mother died?"

The words froze Jorge in his place.

Finally he spoke.

"I wasn't going to." Jorge said. "I didn't have to. You abandoned her, you abandoned us. You didn't have a right to know."

"Bullshit. I did." He said. "I loved her. You may not believe it but I did."

"You're right, I don't believe it." Jorge said trying to force close the door. "Besides, she asked me not to tell you. She knew nothing good would come of getting you involved again and she was right."

"So that's how it is then? I'm a monster?" His father said, pushing the door open. "Guess you're half monster then, right? Like it or not you're my son and I'm you're father. You come from me."

"I know what I come from." Jorge said, venom dripping from his words. "I come from an abusive piece of shit. Someone who used to make mom's life hell."

"Things were different then." He said. "Things were tougher. The world was tougher. I left your mom cause being with her was suffocating but goddamnit I loved her! I deserved to know that she died!"

"You didn't deserve shit!" Jorge shouted, stepping towards his father. "You abused her and then abandoned her! You traumatized me, you ruined my life! Do you know how horrible it was as a kid to keep Sebastian from your shitty behavior? How it felt to comfort mom at night after you'd slap her? It was hell, dad! Hell!"

His father stood silently. Jorge noticed that he seemed hurt. He didn't care.

"Son," his father said, "I know the man I was. The things I did. I was bad, a bad, bad man. But that's not me anymore. I'm remarried. Her name is Annabel and she's amazing. She changed me for the better."

"I don't care." Jorge said. "I don't care who you are now. You'll always be the man you were."

"So that's it then? My own son doesn't believe in second chances? I gave your mother a million of them."

"You DON'T get to talk about her." Jorge said.

"You don't even know everything."

"I don't need to. I don't care if she cheated on you, broke your heart, fucked your brother. I. Don't. Care. At the end of the day she was here for us. You left. You abandoned us." Jorge said, his heart racing within him.

"There's still time to fix things, hijo."

"I don't want to."

"Maybe you will," his father said, "when you hear about Tenoch."

"I don't even know who the hell that is." Jorge said, preparing another door slam attempt.

"He's your brother."

Jorge stopped. "What?"

"Me and Annabel had a son 6 years ago. His name is Tenoch. He'd love to meet the three of you."

Jorge didn't speak. He didn't know what to say.

"I've told him about his three brothers that he's never met." His father said. "He's asked repeatedly to meet you all. I keep telling him when the time is right, I think now it is."

Emotions welled up within Jorge. It took every ounce of strength to say what he had to.

"No."

"No?"

"No. When he's older he can find me on his own, but I don't want anything to do with you. I've lived for years with your toxicity in my head. I'm through with it. I'd love to meet Tenoch, but not if it means I have to deal with you."

"What about Abel and Sebastian then? Don't you think they'd like to choose for themselves?"

"We have chosen." Sebastian said, stepping from his bedroom doorway. "We don't want anything to do with you either."

Abel and Sebastian walked to stand next to Jorge.

"Our brother has been a better father than you'd ever be." Sebastian said. "We don't need you."

"Yeah," Abel said, taking hold of Jorge's hand, "we'll be just fine without you."

Their father shook his head. "So that's it then?"

"That's it then." Jorge said, finally beginning to shut the door as his father stepped back. "Don't ever contact us again."

As the door finally clicked shut Jorge felt as if he could breathe again. He collapsed to the floor, overwhelmed by his emotions.

Abel and Sebastian kneeled down and embraced their older brother.

The three sat there, holding each other.

It was a feeling of unity. Of strength.

Of brotherhood.

Sebastian X

Sebastian entered the coffee shop apprehensively.

He hadn't been here since he had blown up at Raul and it felt strange to be here now.

Why did I agree to this?

His eyes scanned the restaurant before he noticed him. Sitting in back, where it had happened, was Raul.

As Sebastian walked towards him, Raul stood up.

"Hey! I'm glad you came."

Sebastian hesitated before giving him a slight hug. "Hey. Yeah when you texted I wasn't sure but, I don't know, guess I wanted to see what you had to say."

They sat down amidst an awkward silence before Raul began to speak.

"Look, I'm really sorry. I messed up. Badly. I know this and I've just kept replaying everything in my head and honestly I feel really stupid. I don't know why I said or implied those things about Abel and I'm sorry."

Sebastian paused for a moment before answering back. "Raul, I know you didn't mean to cause any harm with your words but my brothers are the most important things in my life and I just can't be with someone who says things about them."

"I know."

"I liked you, I still like you. But I don't think we can fully go back to what we were. Not yet."

"I understand that completely." Raul said. "I know you need time. Can I say something honestly though?"

"Of course."

"Even if we never get back together, more than as a boyfriend, I miss you as a friend."

Sebastian smiled sadly. "I've missed my friend too."

"And if you still would rather not talk to me I get it. But I wanted you to know how sorry I am. Not just towards you but towards Abel also."

"I appreciate that." Sebastian said. "I'm still down to try to be friends. With a little time, who knows what else will happen."

"I'm glad to hear that." Raul said. "I've been working on being more careful with my words. I don't want to mess everything up anymore. Not just with you, with everybody. I have a tendency to say too much."

"I can tell." Sebastian said with a laugh. "But I know at your core you're good. I just wish things hadn't gone the way they did."

"Aside from watching what I say I've also been looking inwards to some of my own prejudices. Those things I said about Abel...I'm not proud of them."

"They seemed out of character honestly. I've never heard you talk about someone's weight like that."

"I guess it's just something in my brain I need to work out. Enough about me, though. How have you been?"

"Oh boy," Sebastian said, "have I got some stories for you."

***

That night, Sebastian sat outside on a lawn chair looking up at the stars.

There's so many. They feel infinite.

It was such an obvious thing to say, yet it's all that really came to mind. The night air soothed him as he continued to watch them.

With a deep breath he closed his eyes.

He saw his mother. His father. Jorge. Abel. Raul.

People that had entered his life.

Or had he entered theirs?

He sometimes imagined himself as a tornado that stumbled into people's lives unexpectedly.

Even if they knew he was coming, they could never really know what he was like until he was there.

The darkness of his closed eyes brought him comfort.

I am a tornado.

Some things were meant to be destroyed, like his relationship with his father.

Others were still standing even after he had passed through.

Like the love between brothers.

It was a comforting thought. He liked othering himself and seeing himself as a force of nature.

I am Sebastian the Tornado.

Or Seb if you know me well.

He laughed and opened his eyes.

The stars began to dance.

__Abel X__

ONE YEAR LATER

Abel lightly dragged the paintbrush across the empty canvas.

He had already sketched out and mapped what his painting would be, now he just had to execute it.

If he had a natural habitat, it was art class.

"Be sure not to hog all the paint." Thomas said, sliding one of the plastic buckets over. "You got really carried away last time."

Abel smiled and dipped his paintbrush in a vibrant red. "Can't help myself sometimes. An artist such as myself can't be held back."

"Two months into the new school year and you've become a painting monster." Thomas said, playfully shaking his head. "I seem to recall you saying you weren't much of a painter."

"I wasn't." Abel said. "But now I am."

Now 11 years old, Abel had found himself with a much improved school life than the year before. Thomas had ended up in his classes and they got to spend even more time together.

And that wasn't the only big change.

"Save some red for me, dude!" Charlie said, running to pour some on a small paper plate. "You used it all last time!"

"You snooze you lose." Abel said sarcastically before handing Charlie the paint.

His old friend Charlie had returned at the beginning of the school year.

And we picked up right where we had left off.

It felt amazing to have a reunited friend group like this.

The school year before had seemed like a distant nightmare by this point. His life had stabilized and he couldn't be happier.

"You know for someone who didn't stop hugging me for five minutes when he saw me again, you sure like to mistreat me." Charlie said, jokingly.

"Well I was happy to have you back, now I'm happy to hog paint."

Thomas tsk-ed. "See what art does to you? I'm telling you Abel, painting monster."

The boys laughed as the teacher announced that it was time to start cleaning up.

"You guys still coming over after school?" Charlie asked.

"Definitely." Thomas said.

"Wouldn't miss it for the world." Abel answered.

***

Later that day, Abel sat at his desk, doodling into his brand new sketch book.

For days he had been working on a picture of himself, Jorge, and Sebastian. It was all finally starting to come together.

He heard a knock at his door and quickly buried the drawing under some other papers.

"Come in!"

Sebastian poked his head in. "Hey, Jorge told me to tell you that dinner'll be ready in 10 minutes."

"Alright," Abel said, "I'll be there in a sec."

As the door closed, he pulled the drawing back out and continued to work on it.

Things feel so different than last year. So much better.

Life had steadily been improving since their father's reappearance.

The biggest difference (aside from Charlie) had been having Bea in the house. She had moved in recently and, every night, was trying out a new meal.

Jorge's lucky to have her.

We all are, actually.

Everything in the house felt so much lighter. He felt as if he could breathe again. All the sadness was slowly eroding away and, in its place, happiness began to bloom once again.

All my hoping is finally paying off.

He smiled as he put the finishing touches on the drawing. It was easily his best work yet.

But something was missing.

Back to the drawing board.

He crumpled up the paper and started to sketch a new one. This time with Bea in it.

Like my teacher says, an artist is never happy with their work.

Maybe he'd never be happy with his work, but at least he was happy in general.

That's all he had ever wanted.

Jorge X

"So I look nice today?" Jorge asked, checking himself out in the mirror.

Sebastian and Abel rolled their eyes.

"We told you a million times already! You look fine!" Sebastian answered.

"Yeah, don't panic." Abel said. "It'll all work out."

"Easy for y'all to say. You guys aren't the ones proposing today!"

"You really think she'll say anything but yes?" Sebastian asked, getting up to go stand by his brother. "You're just overthinking it. Like always."

"It's a thing worth overthinking. I don't wanna be like on those sad YouTube compilations of rejected proposals."

"Those are mostly fake anyways." Abel said, also standing by his oldest brother. "You'll be fine."

"I don't know how I talked myself into this." He said.

"You did it because you love her." Sebastian told him. "We all do. It's been amazing having her around."

"She's really filled this house with joy." Abel added. "She might be the nicest person I've ever met."

"And yet I'm still a nervous wreck." Jorge said, straightening his collar. "She's gonna know something's up as soon as she sees my shirt."

"Probably." Sebastian agreed. "But it's better than taking her by surprise."

"Why's that?"

"She hates surprises."

"Oh god." Jorge said, head in his hands. "I hope I'm not making a mistake."

"Worst case scenario she says no. Best case scenario she says yes. No point in worrying over anything else."

"Suppose you're right." Jorge said.

"Besides," Abel said, comforting his brother, "she's totally gonna say yes."

***

Okay it's almost time.

Jorge kept looking at the food on Bea's plate. As soon as she was done, he was planning on proposing.

It had been a long, nervous dinner of Bea's signature spaghetti, but the time was almost near.

"Jorge?" She asked, breaking him from his thoughts. "Everything okay?"

He nodded weakly. "Everything's fine. I've just felt so swamped lately."

"With what?"

"Y'know," he said, awkwardly, "just life in general."

She laughed. "What a strange way to phrase an answer."

He looked over to Sebastian and Abel who nodded towards her.

They were right, he needed to get it over with.

"Bea," he said, "there's something I need to say."

He stood up and lowered himself onto one knee.

"Since I've got you back into my life, things have felt so free and amazing. Not just for me, but for Seb and Abel also. You've helped us crawl out of the sad, sad pit we were in and I can't thank you enough. I feel complete now. My life feels complete with you in it."

Tears began to well up in Bea's eyes.

"I guess you know where I'm going with this." He reached into his pocket and pulled out a small black velvet box. "Bea, will you marry me?"

He opened it up and as the diamond shone in the light, Bea pulled him up and leaned in to kiss him.

"Of course I'll marry you." She said.

They kissed again as Sebastian and Abel cheered and clapped.

Jorge pulled away and placed the ring onto her finger. She motioned for Sebastian and Abel to walk over.

The four held each other in a big group hug.

This is it.

This is what I've wanted.

Jorge felt tears run down his cheeks as he stood, embracing his family.

<u>Epilogue</u>

Sylvia Gonzalez peeked into the room of her 4 year old son Abel.

He was fast asleep, breathing quietly in his bed.

Mi bonito. Always such a good sleeper.

She closed the room door and next looked in on 7 year old Sebastian.

As the hallway light shone in, she saw him, limbs wildly hanging over the bed, hair a mess from tossing and turning.

She quietly laughed to herself.

Y mi loco. That boy can't help himself but move all night.

She closed the door and stopped outside the room of her oldest son Jorge. Now that he was 15, he had asked her to stop coming into his room without knocking and she respected that.

Still, she always had that same motherly urge to check in on him and she had to stop herself every night.

So grown now. My little man.

She walked away from his door and sat down in the kitchen. The table was littered with bills but she decided to take a break from worrying about them.

They'll still be there in the morning.

Instead she sat and thought about her boys. It seemed like only yesterday they had been babies in her arms.

Now they were growing up, changing into their own people.

They were nice as babies, but she loved watching them grow into actual human beings. Watching their personalities take shape, glimpsing into their future.

What they would become.

Sometimes she worried but, ultimately, she knew they'd be fine.

As long as they have each other.

Acknowledgements

I would like to thank my whole family who has stood by me and supported me, even when it wasn't easy. I'm able to write the stories I write because of them and I'm eternally grateful for that. Every moment of love, every happy memory created, every light at the end of the dark tunnels in this book is thanks to them.

Special thanks for my mother who has always believed in me and shown me the best life possible. This book would not be here without her.

Finally, this book is dedicated to M, L, G, O, and Y.

Y'all know who you are.

Printed in Poland
by Amazon Fulfillment
Poland Sp. z o.o., Wrocław
03 June 2023

bb8b2494-9ee7-43cb-8984-2bb1b7ac6e65R01